IN SUNLIGHT OR IN SHADOW

May the luck of the Irish go with you

Karen Wilhel

"A J"

On the cover (clockwise from left)

1. Brian Londrow
2. Ted Berlinghof
3. AJ O'Neil
4. Mike Wilhelm
5. Bob O'Neil
6. AJ O'Neil
7. Andy Meisner
8, 9, 10. Pipers
11. One of the many people who helped out

IN SUNLIGHT OR IN SHADOW

How a little café in a little town in Michigan
touched hearts around the world with a
50-hour Danny Boy Marathon

Karen Wilhelm

Ferndale
Press

FERNDALE, MICHIGAN

Ferndale Press
3266 Garden Avenue
Royal Oak, Michigan 48073

First edition

Copies of this book may be purchased at selected outlets or directly from the publisher.
Special discounts are available.

ISBN 9780615266572
10 9 8 7 6 5 4 3 2 1

Book design by Jacinta Calcut
Illustrations and cover design by Joe Simko
Printed in the United States of America

In memory of Sean Fitzgerald, 1965–2009

"My dad sang. I sang. Great time."

CONTENTS

FOREWORD

SINGING ONE IRISH SONG FOR 50 HOURS is quite a feat, but that was the least important part of this story.

The Danny Boy Marathon was more remarkable in the way it brought ordinary people together. You could feel the joy they shared just by hearing in the news about the goings-on at AJ's Café in Ferndale. Those folks had the exuberance of baseball fans whose team has won the World Series.

As I read this book, I was touched by AJ's story of how J.P. McCarthy inspired him to learn the song. I was even more touched when I read how the song took on special meaning for a son and his father, just as baseball so often does.

AJ seems to be a guy who sees the positive side of life, and who is willing to follow his dreams. He draws people into his world. They see his vision and believe that they can accomplish almost anything.

The stories of joy and sorrow told by the people who took part in the Danny Boy Marathon will make readers want to laugh and cry. We all stand in sunlight and in shadow when we journey through our lives, which makes that sentimental song, "Danny Boy," a perennial favorite. People at the marathon stood in the sunlight and shadow together.

I'm kind of sorry I missed that marathon but when I read this book, I felt like I was there.

Ernie Harwell

PREFACE

BUTCH HOLLOWELL, MY FRIEND and open-mic-er, and I were talking about fathers, sons, and baseball. We each had our own memories of listening to Tiger baseball games on the radio on the front porch or in a lights-out living room on a hot August night, before the days of air conditioning. Those memories connect me with my father.

Ernie Harwell was the voice of the Tigers for most of my life. When I think of Ernie, I'm a kid again and Pops is talking to the radio, pleading for the next pitch, and Ernie has us on the edge of our seats. "Come on, come on," Pops is telling Ernie that he wants a double play, or a strikeout, or a Willie Horton dinger as if Ernie is the guy who will deliver. It's a foul ball into the stands and I can hear Ernie's voice today: "A fella from Birch Run got it." I always hoped Ernie would say the fella was from Berkley.

I couldn't resist the impulse to send a copy of the first chapter of *In Sunlight or in Shadow* to Mr. Harwell. I never expected to hear from him, but he called me. He had read the chapter and liked it, and he gave me the name of his friend and publishing mentor, Bill Haney. I guess that made me the fella from Ferndale.

Bill read the chapter. He thought it had possibilities. He met with this book's author, Karen Wilhelm, and me at my café and we started an adventure in "collegial publishing" as Bill calls it.

He helped us through every step of writing and publishing this book, and we're grateful for his guidance and kindness.

I was lucky to get help from Ernie Harwell and Bill Haney—but then, I've had the luck of the Irish all my life. The way the Danny Boy Marathon exploded into a phenomenon talked about far and wide was another example of my great good fortune. I've learned that life comes to me, if I let it, and "Danny Boy" came like a freight train. All I had to do was hop on. It's been a great ride.

AJ O'Neil

ONE

ALONG COMES "DANNY BOY"

AJ O'NEIL FACED THE AUDIENCE. There should have been no reason to be nervous. After all, he was the owner of this music café. But long before AJ came on the scene, Ted Berlinghof's casual Wednesday night open mic had been going on here. AJ was the newcomer.

AJ turned to Ted, who stood next to him ready to accompany him on guitar, and asked, "Do you know 'Danny Boy?'" It wasn't the sort of song people usually performed here, but it was the only song AJ could think of. Ted said, "Sure," with encouragement in his voice, and struck the opening chords.

AJ's voice rang out, just as it had the first time he had sung the song in public at his father's funeral. The words spoke to him of love and loss, joy and sorrow, and the melody lifted him and carried him to the final notes of the song. The audience responded with unexpectedly warm and enthusiastic applause. One man was in tears. "Danny Boy" had just made AJ part of Ferndale's music community.

⁓

ONCE AGAIN, AJ STOOD on the same stage singing the same song. Only this time, a year later, he was bringing a 50-hour Danny

Boy Marathon to a close. AJ felt his father's presence, and his three brothers looked on with pride.

More than a thousand performers, including the governor of Michigan, had taken the stage in the unpretentious café during the last three days, offering endlessly varied interpretations of "Danny Boy," firmly committed to achieving one man's dream. It had become their dream too. Everyone in the crowded room shared the satisfaction of reaching the goal. More than that, they had found connection and community in otherwise separate, even isolated, lives.

The "Danny Boy" magic had carried everyone in the café—and everyone who watched from around the world—to a place of hope, a respite in unsettling times.

⌁

WHY DID "DANNY BOY" RESONATE so strongly with AJ that he would want to hear 50 hours of it? The song had become intertwined with memories.

"Danny Boy" had first come into AJ's life through radio. J.P. McCarthy was the much-loved and respected king of talk radio in Detroit. Anyone who was anyone—local politicians and U.S. Presidents, baseball stars and football coaches, actors and Nobel Prize winners—wanted to be interviewed on the show.

J.P. liked to have fun. He loved Saint Patrick's Day, with its green beer and shenanigans, and he held an annual "Danny Boy" singing contest as part of the festivities. As AJ listened to the show in 1995, he decided he'd be one of J.P.'s cronies the next year. He'd learn the song and enter the contest. Alone in his living room with a cassette tape of the Irish Tenors, AJ listened, sang, rewound, corrected, and finally committed the song to memory. He rehearsed again and again, in the car, in the shower, anywhere he was alone.

When he was ready to sing it before his first audience, his mom and dad, the song gave him an unexpected closeness to his father—Pops, as he called him. "I knew that if I told Pops I had learned a song and wanted him to have a listen, he'd be all ears," AJ remembers.

"Breakfast was on the table when I arrived. I told Mom and Pops that I wanted to sing the song with the bigwigs on the J.P. McCarthy Saint Paddy's Day show. I sang, 'Oh Danny Boy, the pipes, the pipes are calling, from glen to glen and down the mountainside...' I didn't sing out of tune, miss a beat, forget a word or a note. And, until that moment, I had never seen my father cry. He loved it.

"I could see my triumphant entrance into J.P. land. I was on my way to being hailed as one of J.P.'s boys, singing 'Danny Boy' for the greatest guy on radio. Next year, I am in."

But it was not to be. Sadly for all Detroiters, J.P. McCarthy was diagnosed with myelodysplastic syndrome, a form of leukemia. It wasn't long before his plight became public. When doctors thought a bone marrow transplant could help, thousands of people lined up to be tested, but a match was never found.

J.P. held on. For a while, he did his show from home, his entire audience aware that he wouldn't be there for them much longer. AJ says, "I know how comforting it was for me to hear his voice. But as time went on, we heard him less and less. J.P. had always brought us the news, and then he *became* the news. I listened intently for reports on his condition as it worsened."

J.P. McCarthy died on the afternoon of August 16, 1995, with his family at his bedside. Detroit had lost an icon. Tributes came from people who knew J.P. or had been interviewed by him, including former President George H. W. Bush.

"No longer would Detroiters wake up with J.P. in the morning," says AJ. "No longer would he show us all how to celebrate Saint Patrick's Day, and no longer would I look forward to singing on his show. 'Danny Boy' got put in my back pocket. I had no idea how long it might stay there."

OPENING DAY AT TIGER STADIUM had been as important on J.P. McCarthy's calendar as Saint Patrick's Day, and Pops shared that enthusiasm. He raised his four sons on baseball. They went from baby bottle to baseball glove. There was only one team Pops loved more than the Tigers: any team one of his boys played on. He found a way to get to all of their games.

The evening of June 25th, 1996 was perfect for baseball. The O'Neil brothers were young men now, all on the same team. Pops could see them all play without having to go from field to field. AJ says, "I was pitching. Brian, my older brother, played shortstop. Dennis, one year younger than me, was at first base. Bobby, the baby of the family, was in the outfield. I saw Pops walking toward the field from the parking lot. He stumbled. He looked tired."

AJ's father's health had been precarious for much of his life, and the family knew that heart disease, high blood pressure, and ailments resulting from a childhood bout with rheumatic fever could take him at any time.

"I don't remember if we won or lost that night," AJ says. "No one cared. We all played and Pops got to see us. That's all that mattered. That evening, my father went to sleep on the couch and never woke up. Mom found him, and stayed beside him through the night."

Brian came to AJ's house the next morning. "Pops died last night," he said. "Mom wants us to come before the coroner takes him away."

"There we were," says AJ, "all of us, on the floor with my mother, saying goodbye to our dad. His body was cold, but there was still a smile on his face. We told him that we loved him, each of us in our own way, then we wept together. He had finally had enough and had gone to sleep. Brian became the patriarch that day, and we looked to him for guidance as we made the funeral arrangements. Hundreds of people would come to see Pops at the funeral home, people that I never realized knew him. I was surprised and touched as I saw how many people cared about him."

The funeral mass would be conducted at Our Lady of La Salette, AJ's father's church. Brian wanted to give the eulogy. He asked if any of his brothers wanted to add anything, and AJ could think of only one thing, to sing "Danny Boy."

"With all of the details to get together," says AJ, "I never had time to rehearse with the organist. I met him for the first time when the priest announced my name. The church was full. So many people had come to his funeral that the Berkley Police Department had given the procession an escort from the funeral home to the church.

"A lifetime of memories went with me as I walked to the front of the church. All those times that I thought that I knew better than my dad, that he was old fashioned, that he could have done a better job, that he could have been a better father. He had done all that he could, and then some. With very little money, he kept a roof over our heads, fed us, and protected us. He gave us all of the wisdom he had. In the last few years of his life, when we would part, instead of saying 'goodbye,' or 'good night,' or 'see ya later,' Pops would say, 'I love you.' At first, it was scary. After a while we got used to it. It was nice to hear.

"I loved him dearly and I never got to tell him. I was sorry I never thanked him, or let him know that I felt that he had done a remarkable job in life. As I went up to the podium to sing, those were my thoughts."

The organist whispered, "What key?"

"I don't know what key. I only know how to sing the song."

The organist told AJ to start singing. He would find the key and join him.

AJ began, "Oh Danny Boy..." He sang quietly but forcefully.

"I sang," he says, "but I heard no organ. What had I done? Am I off key? Should I stop? I kept singing—still no organ, but I couldn't stop."

AJ heard people crying, but held his head up as he sang, holding back his own tears. He could not cry, not now. He felt that his father was with him. AJ says, "I'm sure that his love lifted me as I sang. I did not forget any words. I sang the entire first verse, then the second, but never did the organist play. When I finished, I whispered to him, 'What happened?'"

The organist was nearly in tears, and told AJ that the singing had been too beautiful to interrupt.

AJ'S COUSIN, LARRY SCHIMMELL, recalls the day. "One of my favorite uncles had died—Uncle Al—the uncle who always had time to sit and talk with you about life, sports, and the Tigers— he loved those Tigers. It was sad; he was young and always battling illness, even though he would never give any indication he had health problems. He was Uncle Al, always with a beaming smile, always upbeat.

"I remember the funeral procession to the church. There were a few near collisions because the Red Wings were battling for the Stanley Cup. Everyone had a Red Wings flag on their car, and the funeral flags stuck on our cars blended right in with them. Then again, everyone was an Uncle Al fan, and I'm sure he was looking down and loving it, his funeral procession mixed in with a bunch of sports fans.

"At the end of the Mass, they said someone was going to sing. When I realized it was my cousin, I was shocked. I can still see myself in that church looking at him and feeling embarrassed for him. AJ can't sing, can he? Well, needless to say, AJ can sing and he sang brilliantly that day. After all the crying in the church subsided, I was embarrassed for myself because I never could have done what he did."

AJ DID NOT SING "DANNY BOY" again for a long, long time.

Two

Soup for You

AJ LITERALLY FELL INTO HIS CAREER as a café owner. The day after Pops's funeral, he went back to work as a self-employed roofer. His brother Dennis was his only employee. One afternoon, as a storm bore down on them, AJ was 35 feet off the ground on a ladder Dennis steadied for him. In a rush to get down before the storm hit, AJ tried to grab a tool that was just out of reach. As AJ realized he had taken one too many risks, the ladder pitched backward.

He smashed into the side of a pickup truck, then hit the concrete driveway. He broke his left arm, ruptured his Achilles tendon, demolished his ankle, blew out a kidney, and broke six or seven ribs. At the hospital, surgeons raced to save the arm, replacing an artery with one from his leg. Had he struck his head, his family would have been holding his funeral, ten years after his father's, instead of gathering in his hospital room.

"I didn't have any insurance," AJ says, "so three months later, I was back on a roof trying to make a living." Doctors told him to find a job on the ground. But what would it be?

One idea came from Jerry Seinfeld's TV show. AJ says, "The 'Soup Nazi' would get angry at someone in line at his restaurant and shout 'NO SOUP FOR YOU!' If for nothing more than the slogan, I liked the idea of opening a café and naming it 'SOUP FOR YOU!' In my neon sign, I would have one unlit word in front of that, so that when I was closed for the night, it would say, 'NO SOUP FOR YOU!'"

ALTHOUGH THAT THOUGHT WASN'T A PLAN, pieces began to fall into place. Branden Reeves was working behind the counter of a coffee shop. Tall and good looking, with a café au lait complexion, and 20 years younger, he captured AJ's attention, and they became a couple.

Branden Reeves and AJ O'Neil.

"Branden and I were walking in downtown Royal Oak and we came across a boarded-up Coney Island hot dog place. It was the perfect spot for my café. I called my attorney and he drew up a lease agreement. But when I showed up for my appointment with the landlord, he didn't. He had sold the place shortly after we made our verbal agreement. No 'SOUP FOR YOU.' It was back to roofing."

Then one day AJ got a call from his attorney. Was he still thinking of opening a café? There was one for sale in Ferndale, not as desirable a location as Royal Oak, but one that seemed like it might be emerging as the next cool place.

The business for sale was called Xhedos, a coffee house and vegan café with live music and a loyal clientele. AJ says, "It seemed to me like a turnkey setup. By April 1st—yes, April Fool's Day—I was the new owner. Me and all of my credit cards had just signed on the bottom line."

The former owner, Caleb Grayson, reassured customers in his MySpace page, "When I told AJ about the history of Xhedos and my original vision, he was in total harmony. For years he's been wanting a place where he could serve coffee and home-made soups. So Xhedos has been saved by AJ O'Neil. It won't be called Xhedos anymore, but it will fulfill the role it has had for the last 11 years, as a community space for a unique town and group of people."

"The first time I walked into the café that would have my name on it," says AJ, "I saw it the same way I would if I were doing a home rehab. I repainted the hideous gray walls with whatever paint I could find at the café or in my basement. Now reds and yellows brighten the place. Beige or white paint add some light to dark corners. My brother Bobby laid new tile in the bathrooms. We have some new seating and some new counter space. AJ's

Café still looks a lot like it did before I took over, but we keep making small changes everywhere. We have a lot of things on our wish list. We're after progress, not perfection."

At AJ's Café

WITHOUT A MARATHON GOING ON, how would you discover the café? Well, if you're strolling down the sidewalk, as many people do in Ferndale, you'll come across a brick-red storefront. It would be easy to walk right past it, but you're at AJ's Café.

In the warmer months, people will be relaxing and chatting at the tables set off from the sidewalk by a black wrought-iron railing. On busy nights the sidewalk tables will be crammed with smokers and those cooling off from the summer heat and humidity. In bad weather, the smokers will be huddled close to the building.

Inside the café, floor-to-ceiling plate glass windows collect the sun on a clear day and people congregate in the window seats to soak up the warmth. AJ's wish list includes a storefront awning and window treatments. On sultry summer nights you might want to add a bigger air conditioning unit to the list. But people say the ambiance is right out of Seattle, or San Francisco, or New Orleans, or Key West—power-guzzling refrigeration would not be right for AJ's.

The performers who sweat through a set under the stage lights will build up a thirst for a cool smoothie or an iced latte, like water ladled out to a prison laborer in a Johnny Cash chain gang song. It's part of the experience of being in the limelight, whether it's on a bayou in New Orleans, the open air of Sloppy Joe's in Key West, or AJ's Café in Ferndale, Michigan.

The entertainment area is on your left as you enter AJ's front door. Tables, relics from a defunct coffee shop in Royal Oak, date from the late nineties. Folded up napkins or scrap paper are shimmed under the tables' feet to keep them from being tippy. Cheap plastic mirrors cover the tabletops to hide the worn and split wood veneer. Another item on AJ's wish list—new furniture.

At the rear is the stage, painted black. Its sound system is temperamental. Sometimes a mic works. Sometimes it doesn't. Whoever is sitting at the controls of the soundboard, squeezed into a corner, has to cope with plenty of uncertainty. An upright piano, painted with sixties' psychedelic swirls of color, stands at stage right. This small space is the home of three open mics every week, special entertainment events, political rallies, and would one day be the spot for an event AJ could have scarcely dreamed was in his future.

Place your order at the counter

IF YOU COME TO THE CAFÉ for a cup of coffee or something to eat, turn right as you enter the front door and you'll find the glass-topped counter, probably with AJ behind it dispensing a hot or cold drink or a spirited opinion. The counter is covered with sign-up sheets for upcoming events. To be an authentic AJ's Café sign-up sheet, it must be handwritten and coffee stained.

Behind the counter are the espresso machine, coffee grinders and coffee pots, perpetually brewing either AJ's "Ferndalian" breakfast blend, dark and bold "Legal Colombian," or "Unleaded" (decaffeinated). Spiced cinnamon pumpkin or chai lattes and milkshakes are other favorites, especially the vegan chocolate-peanut butter-banana shakes.

From this station AJ yells out the orders to his brother Dennis in the kitchen area just out of view. AJ shouting, "I'll take a mexi-tofu roll-up, for here," is nearly always followed by a "What?"

followed by AJ repeating the order, followed by an "OK" from Dennis. It's Dennis's way of making sure they've got it right.

AJ talks about the café with affection, "Dennis, Branden, Sean, Jason, and I all work together. We all do things a little differently. Recognizing that and respecting it is important, so long as it does not affect the quality of the product. AJ's is not a place where you'll find dress-alike clones. Some people say that I make the best smoothies; others say no one makes a better vegan "milk" shake than Dennis does. Branden insists that it is unanimous that he makes the best lattes. We all agree that Sean makes the best hummus and Jason makes the best veggie chili. It's all good."

Small tables line the wall opposite the counter, where "Type A" people, who thrive in noise and need it to get something done,

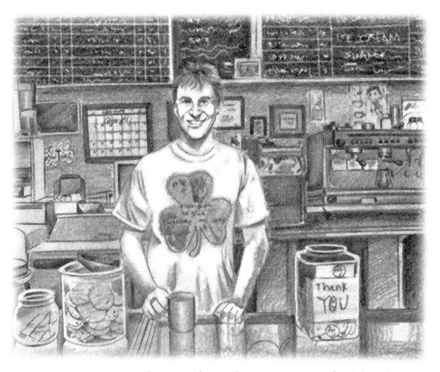

AJ has a knack for making his customers his friends.

sit in front of their laptops. Many customers will come in to study or work or to just be creative because AJ's Café inspires them, whether it's because of the background noise, an over-heard conversation, a piece of new art on the wall, or a freshly authored folksong.

The wooden floors throughout the café are darkened and worn by the countless feet that have tramped across them since God knows when. AJ plans to sand and refinish them. He believes the off-white paint on the pressed-tin ceiling doesn't do it justice, and envisions it one day in bright yellow, with emerald green cove moldings, and a chandelier. Put that on the wish list.

Turning back to the counter, you look up and see the menu on a chalkboard that spans the wall. There are vegetarian and vegan items as well as chicken, turkey or ham sandwiches, or even BLTs. Spicy homemade soups are always available. Roll-ups—spinach tortillas with fillings like tuna salad or grilled chicken—are popular. So is the hummus plate, with its fresh carrots and celery. Bagels, muffins, and cookies are there to tempt you. Coffee and tea. Exotic smoothies. Lattes. Iced lattes. Or a tiny cup of perfect espresso.

Parking is in the rear, and don't be lazy about feeding your parking meter—the parking police are vigilant. People come loaded with quarters to feed the parking meters or ask AJ to make change. There is not a regular visitor to downtown Ferndale who hasn't overstayed, only to return to his car to find a ticket.

THREE

OPEN MIC NIGHTS AT AJ'S CAFÉ

"MY VISION WAS TO BUILD a thriving eatery and coffee place," says AJ. "I thought I was prepared for the challenge—Branden had café experience. I could cook. I had experience running a business. I was outgoing and liked people."

But the kitchen was small and lacked ventilation, so AJ couldn't cook as much as he'd expected. He had a stage, but knew nothing about the sound system. He was used to selling roofs and renovations at thousands of dollars each, not coffee and sandwiches at a couple of bucks apiece.

AJ says, "People weren't coming in at nearly the pace that I had hoped for. I was disillusioned. I wondered why we weren't bringing in more business."

"Listen to what your customers are saying," AJ was told, "They will lead the way." They led the way all right. "Bring back the music," they said.

"Music and entertainment were not my area of expertise," AJ admits. "I brought in a guy to do the bookings and manage the entertainment, and someone suggested that I get in touch with Ted Berlinghof, who used to host open mic nights at Xhedos."

When he met AJ, says Ted, "I took to him right away. He's open and friendly but he was totally busy with opening the place. When we talked about the open mic, he liked the idea and wanted me to talk with his event manager. When I talked to him, the fellow was like, 'OK, oh gee, well maybe we'll have an open mic, but I think what we're going to do is have one night of rap, that's it, we're going to have a night of rap, and I think we're going to have slam poetry.' Slam poetry, he really loved that slam poetry. He said, 'Why don't you write a proposal?' So I wrote up a proposal. Sent it over to the person. He was like, 'Well, I, I, I think we're going to have open mic once every two weeks. Yeah, every other week, yeah, that's what we'll do, and then we don't want you to have any poets. It has to be all music. No poets, because see...' and I'm going, 'OK, I'll tell the poets that they can't come up.'

"There were all these rules and regulations. I did it for three or four weeks and got to know AJ a little bit better. People started to join the thing, and I said. 'It's kind of tough for the folks to come one week and not come the next. Maybe we should have this every week.' AJ said, 'I'll talk to my guy.' Sure enough, about a week later, AJ said we're going to have it every week. And about a month later, his event planner was gone."

Open mic nights at AJ's Café were born. At first, just a handful of his fellow musicians and friends joined Ted, then word started to get out that music was back in downtown Ferndale. AJ began to feel like open mics held some promise.

Ted says, "After awhile AJ saw that people liked the open mic night, so he brought in other hosts for Tuesday and Thursday. The Xhedos crowd just went back to having music the way they'd had it before, and AJ just had to go with it."

GARY SENICK, ONE OF THE MUSICIANS who plays at the open mics, says, "People were sorry to see Xhedos go. AJ had a lot to live up to. I went back to see what Xhedos had turned into, and was pleasantly surprised."

"AJ was the right person to take over. He kept it a center of Ferndale and the musical community, but he also brought his own unique quality to it, his own personality. That helped to make it even better than it was, and that's a statement, because it really was a cool place. He brought some of the same people back, and he brought new people. It has a new dynamic because of AJ.

"It all spirals back to what's in AJ's heart. It's different from just running a business. It's what you bring to it. It's not only the nuts and bolts; it's your attitude toward your business and the people who come to it.

"His spirit is so good. He genuinely likes people. He's not just in it to make money. He's in it for the greater good, and that is the key. He's a warm affectionate person, with a really good heart, and everything grows from that."

> *AJ says, "I've learned from my customers that their openness and desire for community was here long before I showed up. All I had to do was welcome them. They're the reason we can do things at AJ's Café that wouldn't seem practical anywhere else. Like a Danny Boy Marathon."*

"I STARTED TO GO TO MORE OPEN MICS when this new guy, AJ, showed up," says Ferndale resident Greg Sumner. "His enthusiasm was infectious, his hospitality sincere, and I really felt welcomed in the place. It seemed like a mom-and-pop establishment with a true heart and a true community mission. He's a smart entrepreneur as well, and a born promoter.

"I was learning the guitar, and I like to sing. I'm one of these amateur wannabe musicians, who at the age of—let's just say in my middle age—finally decides to try doing some things in front of people. I found it such a welcoming atmosphere, and to me, that was a combination of AJ, with his vision, his sincerity, and his energy, and, on Wednesday nights, Ted and his warmth and nurturing of amateur musicians."

APTLY NAMED, TED BERLINGHOF is a burly Teddy Bear of a guy with a sixties' mustache. When Ted is the host, no one needs a lot of talent or experience. They just need to love music. Many of the performers who came back week after week had first been coaxed onto the stage by him. They would gain confidence as the audience followed Ted's lead and showed appreciation for their effort, even if it was unimpressive at first.

After watching others muster up courage to take the mic, AJ himself began to feel the urge to perform on his own stage. After the open mic had gone on for a month or so, AJ asked Ted, "Is it OK if I sing at your open mic?"

"You're the owner," Ted replied, "Of course, you can sing."

Later that night, AJ stepped close to Ted at the soundboard and asked, "Is it OK to sing now?"

"Sure!"

On the stage, AJ asked Ted, "Do you know 'Danny Boy'?

Ted says, "We did it together and it sounded great."

The making of a performer

AJ MAY SAY THAT HE WAS a bit tentative about his early performances of "Danny Boy," but he wasn't as shy about performing as he suggests. His mom, Annie O'Neil, says that when he was a small boy AJ would get up on the cocktail table and belt out Christmas carols when she sang them with her sons. And he could be a show-off. When his older brother brought girls home to meet his parents, AJ would entertain them, singing and doing somersaults.

His fourth-grade teacher selected him to emcee a school music performance. AJ says, "I introduced each song, rushing up to a microphone at the front of the stage, then scurrying back to my place among my fellow singers on the risers. Then came the song, 'Bad, Bad, Leroy Brown.' My teacher had told me to ask the audience to clap to the rhythm as we sang. I began, 'Now we will sing "Bad, Bad, Leroy Brown." Please clap.'"

The crowd obeyed his request with laughter and applause. He was stunned and bewildered, but went home knowing he had made people laugh, even if he didn't know quite how.

He got laughs that same year when he played one of Queen Isabella's knights in a play about Christopher Columbus. His mother had made the costume, complete with a helmet, out of a cardboard box and aluminum foil. "Seemed fine to me," says AJ, "until I brought it to school on the day of the play. My classmates burst into laughter when I walked backstage with it on. They said I looked more like the Tin Man in the *Wizard of Oz* than a knight."

Curtain time drew near. AJ was furious. There was no way he was going on stage to be mocked. But his teacher would hear none of his complaints. She asked him how he thought his mother would feel if he went onstage without her creation. He relented and, while he got the laughter he expected, he learned something about mothers.

AJ did have the last laugh. That Halloween, he went trick-or-treating as the Tin Man.

WHEN AJ THINKS ABOUT PEOPLE who have the desire to be in the limelight, but run into obstacles before they get the chance, he says, "How many folks have been in the fourth grade play, played in the school band, or have sung in the shower with dreams of stardom? How many have been on stage in some school auditorium, village theater, or coffeehouse?

"Reality intrudes on our dreams and we join the rat race instead of the Rat Pack, and those dreams fade away, replaced by worries about the gas bill and the kids' new shoes.

"No one knows we are walking among hidden stars who might rival Brad Pitt, Denzel Washington, Sigourney Weaver, and Julia Roberts. We are walking among the could-have-been Bob Dylans and Sinead O'Connors and Yo Yo Mas working in factories, behind desks, and in clinics.

"When they get a chance to shine, if only for an open mic night or a Danny Boy Marathon, they release that pent-up and nearly forgotten talent. And they need to share that talent to keep that dream alive and to affirm to themselves that, but for another bill to pay or mouth to feed, they would be in the lights. When they grace us with a performance at AJ's Café, I applaud them mightily.

"I am not alone in my appreciation for the misplaced stars out there. That was part of the magic that made the Danny Boy Marathon a success. Some of our performers had yearned their whole lives to be in such a place, and the marathon gave that to them. For many of us, the applause and warm reception from an audience of strangers fulfills a lifelong dream.

"Wasn't it Andy Warhol who said everyone gets their 15 minutes of fame? The marathon gave that to hundreds of people."

"Danny Boy" takes hold

AJ's OWN FAME GREW as he became known for his heartfelt renditions of "Danny Boy." Greg Sumner remembers, "It became almost a ritual that at the end of open mic night on Wednesday, AJ would come up and do 'Danny Boy.' At first I thought it was kind of a joke, but he would do it week after week. I could see the sincerity he was selling it with, and I thought, 'Wow, he is serious.'"

The magic of "Danny Boy"

The identification of "Danny Boy" as a traditional Irish song has been questioned, detractors pointing out that the words were written by an Englishman. The ancient melody, on the other hand, is an example of how Irish culture, myth, and legend have survived centuries of attempts to subdue and supplant the rebellious people of Ireland.

It was during the English occupation in 1609 that the lands of the O'Cahans were confiscated. Legend has it that the clan's chieftain, the blind harper Rory Dall O'Cahan, wandered late at night by the side of the river Roe, a bit the worse for drink. He lay down in a hollow and slept, waking to the sound of the fairies playing a beautiful melody on his harp. When he went back to the guests at his castle, he played it for them. It became known then as "O'Cahan's Lament," and later as the "Londonderry Air," then as "Danny Boy."

"One Wednesday night," says Ted Berlinghof, "we were ending the open mic and AJ hadn't sung 'Danny Boy' yet. People were saying, 'We have to go find him.' We couldn't end until he sang 'Danny Boy.' It had gotten into our blood.

"Somewhere along the line, AJ started talking about this marathon, and I thought at first, 'Yeah, right,' but I was learning that when AJ says something, he means it."

As beautiful as "Danny Boy" might have sounded, after hearing anything every week, who wouldn't tire of it? People were asking AJ, "Will you ever stop with the 'Danny Boy'?"

December 7th was AJ's father's birthday. "I rarely go to the cemetery to visit him," says AJ, "even though I go past it on my way to work every day. This time I wished him a happy birthday as I drove by. Singing 'Danny Boy' every week made me think of him often, and I'd dedicate tonight's performance to him. People might be getting tired of it, but they'd hear it at least one more time.

"That night, when someone suggested that it might be a good idea for me to add another song or two to my repertoire, I wondered what I could do to give 'Danny Boy' a fitting finale. I didn't want to just stop singing it and leave it hanging. So, after I dedicated the performance to Alfred James O'Neil, my father, I told the crowd, 'We'll have a marathon. We'll all sing the song come Saint Paddy's Day. Then we'll put it to rest.'"

AJ found a 2008 calendar. March 17th would fall on a Monday. He remembers thinking, "We could start at 3 pm on Saturday, March 15th, and go straight through until 5 pm Monday, Saint Patrick's Day. We would have the whole weekend, which should make it easier to get people to sign up. 50 hours sounded right somehow. I did some quick calculations (which I discovered later were wrong) and figured we would allow five minutes per performance of the two-verse song. 20 songs per hour times 50 equals 1,000 performances. Perfect."

The next day AJ grabbed a piece of paper off the counter— probably the back of somebody's flyer—and wrote, "LET'S MAKE HISTORY—Sign up to sing in our Danny Boy Marathon." He drew lines for people to add their names and contact information.

"I had thrown down the gauntlet," he says. "Now to wait and see if anyone picked it up. There it sat, right on the coffee counter, where people would have to see it. And, sure enough, people started asking about it. I'd pitch the thing and give them the background. After a couple of hours, I had eight or ten names on the page. It was going well. In the age of emails and lightning-quick correspondence, nothing beats the old fill-out-your-name-on-a-piece-of-paper trick."

Four

Persuasion

AJ O'Neil admits almost with pride that he is a shameless promoter. He can sell. And he sold the idea of the Danny Boy Marathon to countless customers, reporters, and community members.

His instinct for selling emerged when he was a kid, just as his penchant for being in the spotlight had. "Every spring," recalls his brother Brian, "an army of kids wearing team caps and shirts would be out selling candy door to door, at the grocery store, on street corners. Each kid had to sell at least one case of 20 boxes. Every May, I groaned. I can't tell you how difficult it was for me to sell that one case. Some years I would end up using my paper route earnings to buy out the last few boxes I couldn't sell.

"But somehow Allen, as we call AJ in our family, would sell dozens of boxes with ease. Every year he sold enough candy to win prizes like baseball gloves, a bike, or a fishing pole. We would leave the house together and go selling on opposite sides of the same street, and he would be all sold out before I could sell two boxes. He just had the knack. One time he persuaded me to walk into a corner bar—we were maybe nine or ten years old—and I thought for sure we would be thrown out of the dark, musty place. But no, he sold a half dozen boxes to hungry drunks.

"He would also seem to get the most new customers and the biggest tips from his job as a paper boy. The average number of

paper routes for a kid was two. He had five. Getting new customers for the *Detroit News* earned him Detroit Tigers tickets, bikes,
wagons, movie tickets, footballs, and hockey equipment.

"As teens, we joined the Boys Club of America and when they
had fundraisers, he would smash sales records again. Every time
I hear about his next accomplishment, I can't help but recall how
he could really sell that candy."

AJ MADE GOOD USE of his salesman's abilities and persistence to recruit for the marathon. He asked customers over and over again to
sign up. Like many others AJ worked to recruit, Miko Steinberg
was reluctant. When he told AJ, "Man, I can't sing," AJ would
say, "You'll just mouth the words. I'll sing with you." AJ was also
working on Miko to bring in some other performers. Miko leads
a drum circle on Sunday evenings at the café, so AJ kept telling
him that there had to be something from the drummers.

AJ says, "If I had a nickel for everyone I asked to sing in the
marathon who responded with, 'I can't sing,' or 'I'll clear the place
out with my voice,' I think I could start an investment company.
I kept repeating: ability was not a requirement. I told people they
would probably stick out about as much as when they sing the
national anthem at a baseball game."

AJ DID NOT HESITATE to show people the sort of thing they would
see. Former Dubliner Aoghain Lakes (he says to pronounce his
name A-gone) says, "The first time I met AJ was when I brought
my small stepson to the café. AJ heard my accent. He sang 'Danny
Boy' to us there and then." His stepson was a bit overwhelmed, but

Aoghain told him, "It's OK, it's OK, they're just Americans."

Before the buzz got too loud, AJ would have to head off any objections from Ferndale's city officials. In January, he pitched the event at a city council meeting. At the last meeting before the event, after promising that the world would be watching Ferndale for three days, AJ says, "I sang it, just to show people how easy it was. I was desperate to fill up the master time slot sheet, and by then I was as shameless as necessary to get the word out." Several members of council were less than enthusiastic about musical performances at business meetings, but the crowd appreciated it.

A surprising number of people watch city council meetings on television. Aoghain was one of them, "I saw him on the TV. There's AJ standing up in front of the city council, saying, 'We're going to do this.'"

TED BERLINGHOF RECALLS one of AJ's other methods of getting people involved, "AJ would run into the room and say, 'OK, everybody up on stage,' and we'd practice 'Danny Boy.' We'd have 10 or 15 people howling and screaming as loud as they could, and I'd be hoping we wouldn't blow out the sound system."

"It was developing momentum," Greg Sumner remembers. "By the time the actual marathon started, it had grown exponentially. It seemed to have the most humble origins, a casual kind of commitment, but AJ just ran with it. Just as I had responded to his energy and sincerity, others bought into it too, and enough people did that to make it such a large community event."

NOT EVERYONE THOUGHT MUCH of the marathon's prospects. Kent Koller, the regular Thursday night open mic host, was among them. He says he thought, "Oh, great. 'Danny Boy.' What is AJ thinking? I had never heard of the song before."

Kent recalls how AJ's relentless requests for participation began to wear down the reluctant, saying, "In the four months before the marathon, I would have plenty of opportunity to hear the multitude of musical renditions AJ had on CD. There was constant harassment from AJ to practice the song. I appeased him by playing backup guitar a few times while he sang 'Danny Boy.' However, nothing, and I mean nothing, could have prepared me for the actual marathon."

Despite his early doubts, singer/guitarist Kent Koller spent hours on stage and at the soundboard.

WORD OF THE MARATHON reached well beyond Ferndale and Detroit. AJ received a handwritten letter from Port Huron, Michigan, 40 miles to the north. Ginny Donnellon was the matriarch of a large brood, their ages ranging from a four-month-old baby to Ginny herself in her seventies. The Donnellons so loved the name Danny that they named their children Dan, Danny, Daniel, Michael Daniel, Daniella, and so on. The entire family of thirty would participate in the marathon. They would perform a number of different renditions, including one with kazoos.

ANOTHER BOOST CAME from Scott Cleven, director of the Saint Patrick's Senior Center in Detroit. He hoped to attract support for his center, which housed, clothed, and fed seniors and homeless people in one of the hardest hit parts of Detroit, and he would also provide a small crowd of performers—a busload of seniors.

Scott says, "I heard that some guy was going to have a three-day Danny Boy Marathon. At first, I thought that sounded crazy, then a light bulb went off—'Danny Boy'—Saint Patrick—sounds like an opportunity. Our grant funding has been cut significantly over the past three years and I am always looking for new ways to raise funds."

That made AJ see that the marathon could do more than just get people singing. He could ask them to open their wallets to some good causes.

The Detroit Together Men's Chorus—AJ is a member—has been performing for more than 25 years. AJ says, "I wanted them to get some much-needed help too. Volunteers from the chorus would later help with everything—ushering, manning the T-shirts sales counter, handing out certificates of completion and green carnations, and performing. I don't recall any part of the marathon where at least one person from the chorus was not helping."

And with more people finding it hard to make ends meet, AJ

felt the Gleaners Community Food Bank, which has a pantry in Ferndale's Zion Lutheran Church, would be a good choice. With gratitude, the church helped promote the marathon and sent its choir to perform.

As the marathon approached, AJ would give progress reports on the marathon to anyone who would listen. Miko Steinberg recalls, "AJ would say, 'Hey man, we just got a commitment from blah blah blah,' or 'You wouldn't believe who we've got a commitment from now.' This thing was really getting some wheels. I saw it go from a concept to an idea, to a plan of action, to the pulling together of a vast family."

AJ's circle of friends, customers, and neighbors were beginning to believe in the Danny Boy Marathon, but no one could have guessed that the excitement would reach around the world. The pipes were calling.

AJ wanted the marathon to be recognized by The Guinness Book of World Records. Following instructions on the Guinness website, he registered, then received an email with ten pages of guidelines and a form to fill out.

"We filled out the form," says AJ. "and sent it back. Their reply: 'Not interested.' They thought we were going to get a thousand people together to sing "Danny Boy" in a group—the sort of thing people propose all the time—and call it a record."

A friend who holds the Guinness record for the longest solo singing performance told AJ he should hold the marathon, and reapply afterwards. AJ decided to follow his advice.

FIVE

THE PIPES, THE PIPES ARE CALLING

THE MORNING AFTER THE BIRTH of the Danny Boy Marathon, Steve Neavling, a regular customer and a *Detroit Free Press* reporter, walked in. He ordered his soy latte and looked down at the coffee counter. The Danny Boy Marathon sign-up sheet, now on page two, caught his attention.

Steve is a morning guy and not usually around for the evening open mics, so he was one of the few who hadn't heard AJ sing "Danny Boy." Right away, he wanted to be part of the marathon and perform the song on his ukulele. AJ says, "He asked me what had given me the idea to do it and I told about singing it for my dad. I told him I'd been doing it at the open mics to the point where it had almost become a joke.

"It was then that Steve said he thought the marathon would make a great story and that he'd talk to his editor. Days went by. Steve made his morning latte stops and I kept him up to date on the marathon. 'We're on page four now,' I said, pointing to my growing list of names. Finally he said his editor had given him the OK."

The article appeared on page one of the local section of the Sunday, December 30, 2007 issue of the *Detroit Free Press* with the title, "From Glen to Glen to Ferndale; Next: Fifty Hours of 'Danny Boy,'" A web address pointed the reader to a page on the

Free Press website where they would find a video of AJ singing it.

What could be better than to have the biggest paper in Michigan do a story on the Danny Boy Marathon? It had just gone from joke to reality.

～⁀

BY THE END OF JANUARY, it was time to put together a press kit and go after more publicity. "We compiled as many names of media sources to contact as we could," says AJ. "Branden wanted to email our press packages to them. I thought we should contact people directly by phone.

"I just left the emailing to Branden, and decided to do things the old-fashioned way. I started calling Channels 2, 4, 7, as well as many radio stations. I went back into my memory for anyone I might know in the press. I once lived next door to a *Detroit News* reporter. I'd call her. I was on Mitch Albom's show on WJR radio once. I'd call him. Any lead I could think of, I pursued. I had talked to WDIV-TV anchor Carmen Harlan when she walked her dog in a neighborhood where I was doing construction work the previous summer. I'd try her. I called the local papers, even the Royal Oak *Daily Tribune*, where I had been featured as a kid in the pee-wee baseball highlights.

"I was a shameless self-promoter and got busy shamelessly promoting. My day on the road started early on a brutally cold winter morning. With press kits in hand, I hopped into my truck.

"My first stop was Olympia Entertainment to try to get a sponsorship from Mike or Marian Ilitch, owners of the Detroit Tigers, the Detroit Red Wings, and the Little Caesar's Pizza empire. I never got past the receptionist. She promised to pass on my press kit and gave me a phone number and the name of someone to follow up with. A few days later I tried, but received no response.

"Next stop—down the road a few blocks to the WDIV studios to see Carmen Harlan. I walked up to the door. It was locked, and security cameras were trained on the entrance. I pressed the button on the call box and a voice asked me to state my business. I explained to the box why I was there. The box informed me that they do not accept press kits, nor do they relay messages.

"Then I went to the Motor City Casino," AJ continues. "It sponsors events in Metro Detroit so maybe they would sponsor ours. As soon as I got there and made my request, I was led to an office—the security office. The officer on duty told me to leave my press kit and it would be forwarded to the promotion department, so I did. Weeks later, I got a rejection letter.

"Daniel, a friend and customer, is head chef at a posh restaurant at the MGM Grand Casino. I thought maybe he could get me into some big guy's office. I had a couple of problems when I tried to explain my purpose to the security officers: I didn't know Dan's last name and I couldn't remember which of the casino's restaurants he worked in. The little security guy told me I could just turn around and leave, because they don't allow that kind of thing. The big security guy had mercy, and started naming the posh restaurants in the casino until, voila, I recognized the one Dan worked in.

"They let me in and I got to the restaurant. The hostess was on the phone, so I waited. She finally finished her call and asked me the question I'd been waiting to hear, 'May I help you?'

"I explained who I had come to see and she made a call, and I waited some more. She learned he was in a meeting. I left the press kit.

"I was so exasperated that I needed to sit down for awhile. I found a seat—in front of a slot machine. I ended up donating $40 to the casino. I didn't win any money and I didn't win any sponsors.

"I went after Ford, GM, Chrysler, and other big Detroit companies that day and in subsequent letters and emails. Eventually, the local Ferndale Subaru dealer became one of our $200 sponsors. A foreign car company seized a golden opportunity while the Big Three passed.

"It's funny, nearly everyone asked me to send an email. When I told Branden, he shrugged as if to say, 'I knew that's what they would say.' He was too sweet to say, 'I told you so.'"

BRANDEN STARTED SENDING OUT mass emails. Before long, AJ was flooded with replies from reporters wanting to cover the marathon. In Ferndale, Jeremy Selweski, a reporter for the local paper, *Woodward Talk,* wrote on February 10, 2008, "The owner of AJ's Café in Ferndale is hoping to unite the city under the spell of a single song: the poignant Irish folk tune 'Danny Boy.'" Jeremy said AJ told him he would stay awake for all 50 hours of the marathon, hear every performance, and greet and shake the hand of everyone who came in the door. Jeremy quoted AJ joking, "This could be the end of AJ. I picture myself in a green wheelchair, drooling out of the side of my mouth, muttering fragments of 'Danny Boy' in the loony bin."

Ten days later, in another piece Jeremy wrote, Christina Morgan said prophetically, "These are the little things that make history."

MEANWHILE, 500 MILES AWAY, a stroke of Irish luck was headed AJ's way. A Manhattan pub was preparing to announce its ban on singing "Danny Boy." On March 5, 2008, when Shaun Clancy of Foley's Pub issued his edict, a series of improbable events was put into motion. A New York Saint Patrick's Day story going out on the AP wire was no surprise, but it was hard to fathom why it included something happening in a little café in Ferndale.

That AP story started a wave of international attention. It was published in hundreds of newspapers and showed up on hundreds of Internet news sites worldwide. AJ started to get media inquiries from as far away as Australia and Ireland.

"We hadn't heard the last of Foley's Pub," AJ says. "The Thursday evening before the marathon found me on the phone with a radio station in Seattle and Shaun Clancy from Foley's Pub. Shaun talked about the merits of his ban and I discussed the merits of the marathon. His argument was that 'Danny Boy' was a sad and depressing funeral song that didn't belong in a pub. I said that if anyone could see the electricity and harmony that the marathon was bringing to Ferndale, they would never put the word 'sad' together with 'Danny Boy' again. I got the last word—I sang 'Danny Boy' on the air."

"MY FRIEND GEORGE MAURER in Key West was also part of the radio blitz," says AJ. "One of the times I visited George there, I took him to Finnegan's Wake, an Irish pub, where I persuaded the emcee that I was a famous Dublin singer. He bought it and I belted out 'Danny Boy,' to rousing applause. George—who detests the song—had little choice but to listen and go along with the crowd."

After 30 years as a Detroit labor lawyer, George had moved

to Key West, where he broadcasts a daily Internet radio show from his home. It's called the "Just George Maurer Show." Several weeks before the Danny Boy Marathon, George was in Detroit and did his show from AJ's Café. He balanced his disdain for the song with a public's-right-to-know viewpoint and treated the event with a positive spin.

"Danny Boy" threatened

BEHIND THE SCENES, while the momentum of the marathon was building, AJ was coping with a family crisis. His brother Dennis and Annie, his mom, were both sick.

A few weeks before the marathon, Dennis had a kidney stone attack. It was not his first. Doctors thought infection was setting in, and they tried to pulverize the stone using a sophisticated medical device. It helped, but the procedure had to be repeated a week before the marathon. Even so, Dennis was adamant that he was going to sing.

Then, not long before the marathon, Annie O'Neil's breathing became labored and she began having chest pain. With Dennis ill, and Bobby and AJ at work, she made the 911 call herself.

When AJ arrived at the hospital, his mother was on a breathing machine. He was told she had suffered a heart attack. The nurse in charge, Sandy Cagle, was AJ's former sister-in-law, so he could be sure that Annie would get the best care.

"Sandy told us straight," remembers AJ. "Mom was in the final stages of heart and lung failure and they were doing all they could to stabilize her. There was no way to know what to expect. If she responded to the medication, they could remove her from the breathing machine and be optimistic for a recovery. If she continued to need the machine in order to breathe, her prognosis was bleak. Sandy suggested that we ask her whether she would want to remain on life support or not."

AJ held his mother's hand and asked what her wishes were. "Let me go," she told him. She didn't want to be hooked up to a machine. Brian was on his way from North Carolina to be with her, Dennis was still in the hospital, and Bobby was trying to keep everything else under control.

"That was when I seriously considered calling off the Danny Boy Marathon," says AJ. "Each morning, I got the café up and running, went to one hospital to check on Dennis, then to the other to see my mom. Doctors and nurses were calling me to keep me updated.

"I could feel myself beginning to crack inside. As far along as we were with the marathon, I knew that it couldn't go on without me. I couldn't keep doing this and run the marathon at the same time. I kept this to myself and hoped for the best.

"Then, six days before the marathon, Dennis was well enough to go home from the hospital. Mom started to breathe on her own.

"One evening, right there in Mom's room, I got a call from Rebeka Rhodes from WOMC's 'Dick Purtan Show' to schedule an interview. Mom was thrilled beyond words. Dick Purtan is another radio icon in Detroit, and one of her favorites. I started to feel more confident that the marathon would go on."

Just one day before the marathon, Annie was able to leave the hospital. She and Dennis stayed at AJ's home. Branden, Bobby, Brian, and Brian's wife Patty looked after them between stints of helping out at the café. Calls between home and the café went both ways: "How are you feeling?" and "How's the marathon coming along?"

Dennis made it to the café to sing on Sunday afternoon. "He

was nervous," AJ says, "but I can't help but think of the pride and relief he must have felt that he made it to the stage at all. What a journey he had gone through, what a journey for all of us."

IT WAS DURING DENNIS'S AND ANNIE'S ILLNESSES that the marathon got an unexpected boost of publicity through a regular open mic'er, Butch Hollowell. Although AJ didn't know it, Butch's wife is Desiree Cooper, co-host of the Saturday public radio show, "Weekend America." She was interested in doing a story on AJ and the Danny Boy Marathon. A week before the marathon, Desiree and her recording engineer, John, came to the café. For her story, which she titled "Putting 'Danny Boy' to Rest," Desiree wanted some versions of the song to play during the segment. AJ set up a mock marathon.

Trevor Johnson played "Danny Boy" on mandolin, then Allen Sharako played it on his guitar. The Twelfth Night Singers, a Renaissance madrigal group, sang a rousing choral rendition. Kyle Rasche and his band, "A Stowaway," rocked it. AJ did his traditional version. The show aired nationally on Saturday, March 15, the first day of the marathon.

IRISH PUBLIC RADIO CALLED on Tuesday, March 11, to interview AJ for their live drive-time show. He says, "Now I knew that we were on the verge of a whirlwind. Branden hadn't gotten press releases out that far."

Butch Hollowell's connections resulted
in a story about the marathon on
"Weekend America."

Six

Hammering out the details

AJ HAD "SOLD" THE MARATHON. Now there were hundreds of tasks and details to see to. Out of nowhere, volunteers and workers began to appear.

"I started to see that I was going to have help from a reliable group of friends and believers," says AJ. "Some were people I'd gotten to know through the open mics. Others were regular customers who had become part of the AJ's Café scene. Others were chance acquaintances who were excited by the idea and jumped in to help. The marathon was coming to life."

It wasn't AJ wanting something done and telling someone to do it. Somehow, people were figuring out what needed to be done, how to do it, and communicating that to each other. People came in saying, "There's a hole and I can fill it. I'll do it."

AJ, in the middle of the maelstrom, found himself saying over and over again, "OK, that sounds like a good thing to do. Just do it."

Engineer extraordinaire

KEITH DALTON AND AJ BUMPED into each other at a city council meeting. Keith recalls, "AJ started telling me about the marathon and I quickly saw that in his grand vision, he had no plan for the staging. I volunteered to do it. I pushed my way in and took over."

AJ says, "I didn't ask Keith, with his professional video production background, to get on board. He just told me that I didn't have to worry about the stage. He would take care of everything. In fact, he told me when he started, 'Don't even come over here. I know how to do it.'"

Keith Dalton's video system captured every performance.

Keith looked at what he had to work with. The sound system was good. More lighting was needed. He added it. To keep exiting performers from running into those coming onstage, he built a second set of steps. Yellow duct tape made a giant arrow going up the steps on the right. On the stage, a big arrow pointed to the mic and from the mic there was another arrow pointing to the "down" steps. The stage was cleaned and banners hung.

Keith rigged a video camera overhead. He would record the marathon so there would be complete video documentation of the whole stage and the entire event.

"Keith surpassed any expectation I could've had," AJ says. "He hung twenty banners. He did all the engineering. Built the stage, built the steps, put the tape down, made it all safe, put up the karaoke machine, hung cables for sound and video, all that stuff that I would never have thought of doing. He designed it, planned it, and executed it without fanfare, only because he wanted to. He made everything flow so nicely that I gained confidence just from seeing him work."

Keith paid attention to the littlest things, like making the soundboard easier to operate. Mike Wilhelm, who manned the board many times during the event, says, "Keith took a piece of cardboard and drew a picture of which controls operated which mics. The mics get moved around on the stage, and then you can't tell which controls to slide. All the sound equipment is old. Some of the mics and cables have problems. Only five or six channels work. Keith covered the ones that didn't work with black tape, with a note saying 'Don't use these faders, don't even try.'"

Does anybody know the words?

MIKE ALSO REMEMBERS, "People were asking AJ, 'How does the song go?' There are a lot of versions of 'Danny Boy.' So we stood across the counter from each other and he rattled off some words, and in five minutes our version was written. We got the chords from Ted and added them, and I said, 'I'll bring 50 copies to the next open mic.' A week after that AJ said we needed 50 more copies—the first 50 went in a day. I was printing them on my slow home printer. I would put as much paper in the printer as it would take and go off and do something else. Then come back and do it again. Every week it was 50 more copies, and then it got to be 100 copies a week as we got closer."

"I never thought about lyric sheets," says AJ. "I was thinking I'd write the words on a sheet of paper and if anybody needed them, they'd pass it around. Mike realized that people want to practice, they want to feel comfortable with it, and make it a part of themselves for a while."

Producing the sound

THERE WERE OTHER DETAILS MISSING from AJ's plans. He says, "It never occurred to me that we would need a sound person. I thought I'd just say, 'Turn that little gizmo on, we'll mic it up,' and that would be it. We'd just check on it every few hours."

Ted Berlinghof asked AJ after a Wednesday night open mic, "Do you think you'll need people to run the soundboard?"

"Oh yeah, I guess so."

"Do you think we ought to make a schedule?"

"Yeah, sure. OK..."

So Ted grabbed a piece of paper, drew lines on it, very precisely—he's an architect by trade—and said "Let's see—we have to break it up into eight hour shifts. We've got about nine or ten shifts..." He produced his grid and said, "This ought to work out OK."

AJ asked Ted, "How would you like to take this one?" He pointed to midnight-to-7 am, Saturday night to Sunday morning.

Ted had no choice. He just said "OK."

Mike Wilhelm was there at the time and recalls, "When Ted did that, I thought it was incumbent upon me to do Sunday night. Then we'd have both nights covered." Other open mic hosts and people familiar with simple stage controls signed up to run sound for the other slots. During the long hours of the marathon, when one of those people had done all they could do, there was always someone else to volunteer to take over.

THREE DAYS BEFORE THE MARATHON, Butch Hollowell came in and told AJ he was going to help him make phone calls. AJ says, "Even though performers had signed up and we had been filling in the master time slot sheet, Butch realized we needed to actually verify performance times. Butch stayed on the phone for hours—with his own cell phone." A few other stalwarts from the Detroit Together Men's Chorus made hours of calls too.

PREPARATIONS GREW FRENZIED as the marathon approached, but there was always someone there to step in and help when needed.

SEVEN

LET THE MARATHON BEGIN

A HALF HOUR BEFORE THE DANNY BOY Marathon's kickoff, AJ joined the revelers on the sidewalk. He couldn't guess if a hundred or a thousand people were going to show up to sing during the next three days. He hoped for a thousand, but was ready to sing for as long as necessary if turnout was low.

Girls from the Flanagan-O'Hare School of Irish Dance captivated the gathering crowd.

State Representative Andy Meisner stood ready to say
a few words as AJ opened the marathon. Brian Londrow and
Bob O'Neil looked on.

The girls from the Flanagan-O'Hare School of Irish Dance who had been entertaining the crowd left the "trailer park green" carpet that served as the dance floor, dignitary reception area, and grand entrance. AJ had wanted to invoke the drama of Academy Awards night, and emerald green seemed more appropriate for the occasion than red. Home Depot agreed, and donated the carpet.

You could feel the excitement and anticipation in the air. Photographers were waiting. A podium and microphone were placed in the center of the carpet. It was time to start.

As the crowd gathered, AJ took the microphone. He felt confident as he conveyed the customary thank you's. State Representative Andy Meisner made a short speech.

Then pied piper-style, AJ led the politicians and a contingent of Ferndale firefighters—who had arrived with sirens screaming—through the café to the stage. In the rendition that launched the marathon, AJ sang "Danny Boy." He had sung the song so many times that he had no worries about his performance. "The spotlight was on me," he says, "and I loved it."

AJ then turned to the politicians who had followed him on stage. Andy Meisner and State Senator John Gleason had formed an impromptu team. Andy Meisner remembers, "I was supposed to sing alone, but I saw one of my colleagues, a proud Irishman, John Gleason. John was a little worried about going alone, so we said, 'Oh shoot, we'll do it together.'

"John and I went up there with AJ, and it's a good thing AJ was up there with us, because he might have been the only one with a decent voice. We went for it. I gave it my best shot and had fun with it. It was a fun, wacky thing, one of these once-in-a-lifetime things. How many times are you going to be involved with something like that?"

Next came some of the members of the Ferndale City Council—Scott Galloway, Tomiko Gumbleton, and Mike Lennon. They grabbed Ferndale Mayor Craig Covey, and gave it their all.

Standing next in line were the firefighters—but they needed to get back to the firehouse soon. They wanted to slip off the stage, but AJ told them he wanted them to perform next. He says, "These were some pretty big guys, but I had gotten pretty good at corralling singers and they were already on stage." AJ sang with them, and they did a valiant job.

"I was starting to wonder whether I'd have to sing with every group," he says. But people who had rehearsed and could perform without him were lining up. The Danny Boy Marathon was underway. What lay ahead, nobody knew.

AJ THOUGHT THAT PEOPLE TAKING TURNS, singing, and moving along would just happen, but confusion set in almost immediately. Brian Londrow came to the rescue. With his experience directing large ensembles, including the Detroit Together Men's Chorus, he knows how to move masses of people into position, get them to sing at the right time, and keep a show organized.

Brian recalls, "There was a narrow time frame between performers, and the café was jammed with people. If they weren't organized, we wouldn't be able to keep them moving—especially when there were large groups performing."

Brian came up with an "on-deck" circle for the next six people to go on stage, and ranged through the room with his clipboard to line up the performers, walking sideways through the crowd to find people. He would say, "So-and-so, you're up, and so-and-so, you're up after her." Soon there were eight, ten, twelve, fourteen, sixteen people standing in line behind the six in the on-deck circle.

That began to bring some order to the chaos, but AJ's master time slot sheet wasn't going to do all he expected it to. People scheduled into time slots were late or missing, and volunteers were needed to substitute for them. People not on the schedule wanted to sing. Roaming with his clipboard and keeping in touch with the check-in station, Brian saw that every performer was accommodated and every slot on the schedule was filled.

"Brian's process worked perfectly," says AJ. "I've heard so many people say they got to sing exactly at the time they signed up for. It was unbelievable.

"Brian worked until he couldn't do it anymore. Then we went looking for someone able to handle the madness. We handed it off to one guy who gave the clipboard back five minutes later, saying it was way too much for him. While Brian took his break,

I was the handler but I was always happy to turn the clipboard back to him."

BEFORE BRIAN COULD MOVE A PERFORMER to the stage, the person at the soundboard needed an idea of what they planned to do. That was often Keith Dalton, who says, "The fellows up front logged in, organized, and lined up the performer, who might perform a ca-pella, karaoke, with a piano, guitar, or anything they could strum, blow, hit, shake or speak into. One or all of three mics would have to be live and on stage, so I had to be ready for anything."

Keith would ask each performer, "Did ya check in?"

"Yes."

"What kind of performance are you doing?"

They would tell him.

"Sit down in the on-deck row."

Then Keith would be ready to set up for them. He never got too far away from the soundboard.

AFTER EACH RENDITION, PERFORMERS left the stage and walked through the crowd to the front to receive flowers and certificates. David Schroeter of Schroeter's Flowers had provided buckets and buckets of green carnations, enough to give one to every performer. Then they signed the "sympathy book," provided by the Spauld-ing and Curtain funeral home, and had helped make history.

Performers basked in the afterglow as they lined up at the counter to grab a drink and some food. Some stayed on to find a seat and listen to more performers do the same thing, each in their own way.

IT WAS IMPORTANT TO FOLLOW CERTAIN RULES if the performances were to proceed as scheduled and if the Guinness world record was to be attained. They were posted on a chalkboard on the wall. Keith recalls some of them: "It didn't matter how you did it, as long as you performed 'Danny Boy.' There could be no made-up lyrics or parodies, but the tempo and style were up to the performer. You had no more time than what it took to walk to center stage and start. There was to be no addressing the crowd, although some people did anyway. There was no taking in the greatness of your moment. This was not your moment—it was part of a continuous event. If everyone took time to talk about their 'moments,' the whole thing could crash and burn. For all of the 52 hours I was there, I had one thing in mind—we are not going to fail all those who have gone before."

83-YEAR-OLD JACK GUIREY likes to claim that his family has repeatedly won the "Largest Clan" award in the Royal Oak Saint Patrick's Day Parade that had taken place earlier that day. He had promised to bring his gang from the parade to the marathon, but they were still no-shows an hour after the start. AJ says, "I remember nervously waiting for them to arrive, because they were scheduled to be among the first to perform. Jack had neglected to tell me that their favorite watering hole was also a required stop. But just as scheduled, he arrived with his clan in tow and with a horde of other parade-goers."

FERNDALE RESIDENT CHRIS KOLE HAD A BLAST. "My husband, 11-year old son, and I left the errands and housework behind and headed to AJ's," she says. "The marathon had just begun, and we wanted to check it out. The place was festively green everywhere.

"Danny Boy" was played on keyboards, guitars, pennywhistles, pipes, banjos, saxophones, harmonicas, ukuleles, and kazoos.

There were shamrocks, and green carnations, and folks dressed in their Saint Paddy's Day best. Everyone was smiling and laughing. The press was there, and when AJ wasn't being interviewed, he was all over the place. He and his crew worked tirelessly.

"We sat down, fascinated. Folks were photographing the performers, and the entire marathon was being filmed. The enthusiasm and goodwill were contagious. Each performer was met with hearty applause and warm support. It didn't matter if 'Danny Boy' was sung, danced to, recited or played on any kind of instrument. It didn't matter if a singer could carry a tune. We were all there for fun and frivolity and putting Ferndale on the map.

"We were enthralled. Whole choral groups showed up. Singles and duos waited their turns. A time slot needed to be filled, so I volunteered. Being a McCabe originally, it was fun to sing a song my entire family loved. I had sung it at parties and at my grandmother's funeral. This time was sheer joy."

If you're lucky enough to be Irish, you're lucky enough

AJ says, "Luck was with us all the way through the marathon. When the idea of the Danny Boy Marathon first came up, it was lucky that Saint Patrick's Day fell on a Monday. If it had fallen on any other day, I don't think I would have tried it.

"It was luck that Steve Neavling of the Free Press walked into the café the first day the sign-up sheet for the marathon was on the counter and was inspired to write about it.

"It was also good fortune that Butch Hollowell connected us to Desiree Cooper from National Public Radio.

"We were lucky that an AP reporter wrote about Foley's banning 'Danny Boy' and added a paragraph about our marathon. It was even luckier that it was a slow news day so the story was picked up around the world.

"Saint Patrick must have been looking after us when the Michigan winter broke a few days before the marathon. Snow and slush disappeared from streets and sidewalks.

"The Saint Patrick's Day parade in Royal Oak ended at the perfect time for Irish clans and other parade-goers, including the Irish dancers, to get to Ferndale for the start of the marathon. The luck of the Irish, indeed."

KATHY KITZMAN HAD A PRIME SPOT on the schedule. "I was assigned to play "Danny Boy" on my cello during the 7-8 pm time slot on Saturday night," she says. "When I got to AJ's, I was amazed by the number of people crowded into that small space. You couldn't find a place to sit. You could feel the energy and the excitement in the air. And even though it was only March 15, there was a lot of green in that room. I reported to the organizers and found a corner of the room where I could park my cello case. Then it was my turn. I was number 94. The sound folks got me settled. Then I played my two-minute arrangement. After I left the stage and received my green certificate, I saw that there were many open slots on Sunday so I signed up again."

TED BERLINGHOF CAME INTO THE CAFÉ a couple of hours before he was to begin his late-night stint as host and soundman, wondering how many people had signed up to perform then. "I saw this big glass display case with a huge sheet of butcher's paper on it. AJ had painstakingly put a thousand little squares on it, with the time slots in the left margin. People were supposed to put their names there. While there were a lot of people signed up for the evening hours, there were a lot of empty spaces later. I hadn't put my own name down because I figured I'd probably fill in during the gaps. I looked and—what's my name doing on there? There it is again. And there it is again. AJ had put my name down about a dozen times."

PEOPLE CONTINUED TO JUMP IN and work wherever they saw a need. They became owners of the achievement, and AJ was happy to share it, saying, "You had all these people, and they somehow knew what to do. It was all just happening. Everybody got along. Everybody was happy.

Friends helped out wherever they were needed.

"I did whatever I could to fill in, even where I didn't need to. When I got in somebody's way, they could tell me, 'Get out of here. I don't need you. Get away,' and I never had any problem hearing it. I was like a kid at 'Chuckie Cheese.' There were so many things to do that there was always something to play with if someone else was using the toy I like.

"And it was not like work. I'd stop every once in awhile and say to myself, 'Oh my God, look what we're doing. Oh my God.'"

MARIAN SANDWEISS HELPED PROVE that everyone is Irish on Saint Patrick's Day. She says, "At an open mic, I heard a young man sing 'Danny Boy' for an NPR taping. His voice seemed to carry the lilt of what I imagined to be his ancestors' voices. I knew then that I wanted to sing 'Danny Boy,' but in Yiddish—my heritage.

"When Mom said she would sing it with me, I called the National Yiddish Book Center in Amherst, Massachusetts. Al Grand had translated 'Danny Boy' just two weeks earlier. Al emailed us the translation and we talked. I even taped him singing it over the phone. All three of us got choked up over the last two lines."

Marian and her mom, Bea Sandweiss, practiced every other day. She says, "It became 'our time.' Even if other things in our relationship got rocky—as often happens with mothers and daughters—we had this to do, no matter what.

"Until the marathon, we kept telling each other that it was the process, not the product, and that we needed to get out of our way of judging ourselves, and just offer it as a gift, and a representation of our heritage.

"I was amazed at how Mom took on that 'performance persona' when we hit the stage. There was no stopping her, and it was good to look into each other's eyes, as we had when we practiced at home, and find our anchor there. And we found another anchor, a home, and a feeling of belonging by singing in Yiddish, the mamaloshen, the mother tongue, the language of our ancestors."

CHRIS KOLE COULDN'T STAY AWAY. "Later that night," she says, "I decided to pop back in. The place was rocking. Cold though it was, the front doors were open, and it was crowded inside with patrons. We heard folk versions of 'Danny Boy,' keyboard instrumentals, and 'Danny Boy' on flute, and fiddle, and pennywhistle. There was a call for performers, and once again I was up on stage. I had no family there for me, but everyone made me feel welcome. I signed the log, and claimed another certificate proclaiming that I had sung 'Danny Boy' at AJ's during the soon-to-be famous marathon."

The marathon's "official" wording of "Danny Boy," as opposed what other people came in with, and compared to the karaoke version, made for some awkward moments. Duets or groups might sing two versions at the same time. People would change in mid-word to match what they heard someone else singing. Sometimes different versions just melded together.

LISA HURT SAYS, "I HAD A SHOW NEARBY, and drove like a mad-woman to Ferndale to make my slot, big, heavy keyboard in tow, then realized there really wasn't time to set it up. I didn't know what key it's supposed to be in. I tuned my keyboard down to find the right one and forgot to transpose it. Then AJ came out and said I was a special guest—No worries, I'm a pro, right? I spoke to the crowd, while feeling out the key. Strangely enough, when I sang, it sounded like I had been playing it for years, and went off without a hitch. What a cool thing to be a part of. It was an experience I will always cherish."

"WHEN IT GOT TO BE MY TURN, right when AJ promised," Dan Greene says, "I went up there and I did it, the 108th performance. I felt so good. I listened to 65 or 70 different versions. Each was like a brand new song. Every song evoked an emotion. When Lisa Hurt did her version on the electric keyboard, I just couldn't hold it back anymore. She did the best version I heard. I cried and cried and cried over that."

The karaoke machine

The karaoke machine was a boon and a bane. As the performers sang along, it showed the words, and accompanied those who needed it. Unfortunately, the karaoke version of "Danny Boy" was excruciatingly slow. The funereal tempo, with its preludes and pauses, tended to make the singers uneasy. Some just crumbled.

Each time the operator pressed "play," the song would begin. On the monitor, the green, green, grass of Ireland would appear. After what seemed a lifetime, words would finally appear in white letters. As each word turned from white to yellow, the singer was supposed to sing along. Nerves were shattered waiting for those words to change color. Twitches, strain, or concerned looks appeared on performers' faces. Just when the singer's every nerve ending and vocal chord had been tortured, the green, green, grass of Ireland would return with the flute and the organ and set up the finale. But then the karaoke version repeated the last line: "Tis I'll be there in sunshine or in shadow. Oh Danny Boy, oh Danny Boy, I love you so." More than a few people jumped out of the hot seat early, only to have to make a quick return. Hilarious at times, it was painful at others. Hearing the karaoke version was bad enough. Hearing it endlessly repeated also assaulted the nerves and ears of those who were there for any length of time.

Every time a karaoke version started, the sound person had to leave the soundboard and walk halfway across the room to start it up. Despite all of the technology on hand for the event, there was no remote control with a "play" button. For Mike Wilhelm, "there were times when the karaoke was ornery. You'd push 'play' and it would look like it was going to start, but then it would stop. The person standing there on the stage would have no idea what to do."

In defense of karaoke, Kris McLonis explains, "Keep in mind that karaoke machines are used in bars, and people are too drunk to be able to sing faster. But it was very useful because, face it, if you tried to have enough instrumentalists lined up to accompany the singers, it would have been a disaster."

EIGHT

THE FIRST NIGHT SHIFT

ALTHOUGH THE ATMOSPHERE WAS FUN, and even crazy at times, there was always respect for the song and the performer. Greg Sumner says, "I was there late Saturday night, from about 11 pm. I performed 'Danny Boy' pretty straight, with my fledgling guitar skills. Once I started on the song, I sold it. I bought into it, with sincerity and earnestness. I wasn't holding back.

"Just looking out at the crowd, and seeing how they enjoyed it, I felt like they were lifting me too. This was not a joke, and we were really, truly enjoying it. That was another surprise to me—it was not some big goof on the song. Some people looked very uncomfortable on the stage, as though they'd never done it before, and would never do it again, but they all did what they could do. So I didn't embellish it, I just tried to deliver a straight, sincere version."

DUBLINER AOGHAIN LAKES, one of the latecomers, says, "The first time I got up to sing, it was a bit nerve wracking. I said, 'AJ, the first time I met you, you sang this to me—now I'm getting you back.' But to be a part of something like that, being up onstage with that energy—it was great. I was glad I did it."

MILES AWAY, IN NOVI, MICHIGAN, Stephanie Hall was at a party at the Novi mayor's house. She remembers, "I walked in and there were a bunch of guys on a couch with a guitar practicing 'Danny Boy.' The mayor got on the phone and he called AJ's and said, 'We are calling in our performance.' So everyone got around the phone and sang."

Back at the café, Ted Berlinghof recalls, "A guy holding a cell phone walked out on stage and said, 'I have the mayor of Novi on the phone.' He held his phone up to the mic, and you could hear a whole group singing this little squeaky, 'Oh, Danny Boy...' We turned up the mic, and it sounded like Alvin and the Chipmunks."

TAKING PART IN THE MARATHON was a source of new confidence for many people. Kevin Zanotti said he came at night, "just to give some support, to keep it going at night because that seemed to me like the time that AJ would need it most."

According to Mike Wilhelm, "Kevin didn't go up at first. He hung back until it got late. But he was there supporting everybody and supplying a smiling face."

After Kevin made himself take the stage and sing for the first time, he sang many times more. Once he got past singing it solo, "Singing with Mike, where he was playing guitar and singing harmony, that was different. Some of the versions I did with the guys were a challenge. It's a whole different world when you start harmonizing."

OTHER STALWARTS PRESSED ON. Keith Dalton says, "It dropped from wall-to-wall people to about ten of us. We were committed to keeping the marathon going. That meant all of us took turns singing 'Danny Boy' three or four times ourselves, then joining a group doing it in the style of Elvis, or maybe like Bob Dylan, or the New York Dolls. I sang the song about 30 times."

That was how Keith was heard live on the radio all over the world on stations from Wales, Ireland, Australia, England, and the U.S. from coast to coast. He says, "I would be on stage, staring out at an empty room, chairs askew, knowing that earlier the room had a hundred or more people in it. Someone would walk through the maze of chairs to the center of the room, stop, and throw an arm straight up into the air with a cell phone pointed towards me so the radio station on the other end could do a live sound feed. Throughout the night—when I was not singing live on the radio somewhere in the world—I was cleaning, straightening and prepping a very large room full of chairs and tables for Day Two of the marathon."

Keith Dalton achieved instant fame when his performance was picked up by radio and TV..

IN CONTRAST TO THE CRAZINESS of the afternoon and evening, late at night the only background noise was the whir of the video machine and the buzz of the sound system. But camaraderie was taking hold and the performers fought sleep with creativity. As Mike remembers, "We were constantly trying to think of new ways to do 'Danny Boy.' I did a blues version. I did a rock and roll version with Ted. I did the straight version a number of times. Ted got up and started whistling it. I was standing there with Vi Brooks and Alison Donohue, and I started whistling it in counterpoint, and then Vi and Alison started making bird noises. It all came together beautifully. That was one of the high points."

Ted adds, "I did my own blues version, then I think I did a reggae version. It came around to me again and I did a Dave Brubeck version in 5/4 time. I got out my ukulele and I did the Don Ho. I brought a mandolin and banjo too and played them somewhere along the line. I think there was a violin or something, and we did the bluegrass version. The diehards kept it alive."

The soundman

Kent tells his story this way:

"This was a marathon for fathers to sing to their sons, and hippies to sing with politicians. A marathon for individuals of all levels of talent and musical capability, each with their few minutes of fame.

"This was NOT a marathon for the sound guy—me. I worked 10-hour shifts on the Saturday and Sunday of the 50-hour event. After one of them, I went to a friend's party, and while trying to cool off at the drink table I thought I heard someone say, 'Oh, Danny...' I leaped into a

conversation among four strangers. I said, 'I know this might sound crazy, but did someone here just say "Danny Boy?"'

"They all looked at me and said, 'No.' I was suffering aural hallucinations.

"Going to bed at night was like going to sleep with an evil leprechaun. Send my hospital bill to AJ's Café, please.

"I believe I set a world record myself. I'm pretty sure, although documentation is scarce, I hummed or sang every single harmony for 'Danny Boy' known to man. And not just the pretty-sounding ones. I also did the Cindi-Lauper-meets-Bob-Dylan harmonies. Maybe a little Elvis-meets-Barry-White. Or the screeching weasel.

"I started the karaoke track for 'Danny Boy' about 400 times. That might be a record too. I think you're starting to understand the enormity of it all.

"But that's not all. I also witnessed achievement. I saw tears, especially during a grand presentation from a 50-person choir. There were variations that included a bagpipe trio, a ukulele solo, a sign-language version, pennywhistle, violin, full upright bass, and djembe drums.

"And who is the puppet-master who pulls the strings of my sanity and manic mood swings?

"AJ O'Neil.

"He pulled it off, with generosity. A lot of people did a lot of work for a crazy idea. My job was grueling at times, but AJ gave me food, coffee, and the occasional 'I'm losing my mind' look, which I completely understood.

"And you'll be glad to know I've made a complete recovery from my injuries."

NINE

HALFWAY THERE

EARLY SUNDAY MORNING, Erica Lynn, elegant in dark green velvet, was ready to take the stage, thinking there wouldn't be many people there for her singing debut. But a guy with a TV camera came in, didn't say anything to anybody, stood in the corner, took some pictures, panned around the room, moved up to the stage, got some more footage, and left.

Erica had made the big time. The guy had taped Erica's performance, and Keith Dalton's as well, for a Channel 4 morning show. Still astonished, she says, "They sent it to CNN, and it was on 47 TV stations. It was the first time I ever sang in public. Some people sing forever and never make it to TV."

It was in the midst of the marathon that the press attention reached a peak. There were more live interviews from abroad, and live feeds from Key West, Boston, Saskatchewan, Ontario, and local Detroit stations. AJ did so many interviews that there were times when he had a phone in each hand, up to each ear.

AS THE MORNING ROLLED ON, Dorothy Crawford says, "There were hordes of people. Huge church choirs were coming and going, in and out the back door and the front door. If there had been a skylight, they could have let people down through it. You had to fight for a seat. You almost had to knock somebody aside."

THE CHOIR FROM DRAYTON AVENUE Presbyterian Church was one of the larger groups. Sandra Elling recalls, "The adventure began with a suggestion that the choir participate in the Danny Boy Marathon. Proposing something out of the ordinary to a Presbyterian choir can lead to endless questions: Is this appropriate? Is this kind of activity addressed in the Book of Order? Do 'real' Presbyterians do such things? Should we wear robes? After deliberation, the choir agreed to participate but decided that robes were out of the question.

"When the time came for us to perform, we filed on stage and sang our quiet Presbyterian interpretation of 'Danny Boy' to polite applause. But we had a surprise—a 'ringer' in our midst. Our choir director, professional tenor David Carle, began to sing. When he hit the highest and most dramatic note in the last verse, with absolute control and maximum volume, the audience erupted into wild applause and a spontaneous standing ovation. It was a thrilling moment.

"We came to AJ's expecting to participate in a marathon, but we experienced something much greater—a heightened sense of what makes Ferndale unique—caring people from all walks of life, celebrating community together."

Keith Dalton marvels, "People would watch performer after performer sing the same song over and over. It sounds nuts, but unless you were there, you won't understand. I was there, and I don't understand how the same song done over and over again could be so entertaining."

Choirs filled the room with stirring renditions of "Danny Boy."

CORY QUINN, who you'd take for a well-mannered, gentle line-backer, played "Danny Boy" on the piano in his virtuoso style, wearing a green top hat and a smart green suit.

To see Cory so flamboyant and confident was a special joy to AJ, who says, "Cory had come into the café months before and started to play piano during a quiet time of the day. He was magnificent. When I invited him to play for an open mic, he told me he had never played in public before. I was shocked.

"He was a hit at his first open mic appearance and went on to play often, eventually taking second place out of 34 contestants in our 'Ferndale Idol' competition. Cory came to the marathon with his family and, boy, were they proud. So was I."

AJ'S COUSIN LARRY SCHIMMEL, Larry's wife Shelly, and Larry's sister Sandy Fitzgerald had all witnessed AJ's first performance of

"Danny Boy" at his father's funeral, and came to the marathon to help. Larry says, "When I heard that he was putting this together, I was curious. How could you play the same song again and again for that long? How could you get enough people to do it without serving alcohol? Hard to comprehend but, regardless, I would be there with my wife and sister and we would sing. No problem.

"But it became a problem as the weeks raced by. What version would we sing? How fast could we learn to sing it? Why did we say we would sing? There would probably be only two or three people there, I thought. I've embarrassed myself in front of that many before. No problem."

Larry's sister Sandy was concerned too. She says, "As the time drew near, I started to worry. I went online and listened to different renditions of the song. How would we sing it? How would we sound? Why did we say yes?"

"When we got there—big problem," remembers Larry. "Why would this many people come to a café on a Sunday morning to listen to 'Danny Boy' a thousand times?"

Sandy goes on, "As we walked in the door, a man was calling out our names, 'Next on stage.' There was no way we could go up on stage totally cold. AJ rushed over to greet us and told the man to move somebody else into our slot. He calmed us down."

"AJ rescued us by suggesting we all sing together as a family," says Larry. "He would lead and we would sing behind him."

"When our group took the stage," Larry's wife Shelly says, "AJ introduced us—his cousins Shelly, Larry, and Sandy, and his brother Brian, who was there too, then he proudly announced that the Danny Boy Marathon was at the half-way point."

"We did an admirable job," says Sandy, with satisfaction, "but mainly because AJ was singing with us. When we finished—more applause. I beamed as I left the stage. My stage fright had suddenly turned into a love of the lights and the audience."

Larry adds, "What a great way to sing 'Danny Boy' for the first time. With my family. And next time, I will dedicate a solo to my Uncle Al. No problem."

SOMETIME DURING THAT GIDDY AFTERNOON, a *Free Press* reporter made a video of AJ's partner Branden and Branden's brother Justin singing "Danny Boy." Branden explains, "We got through the first verse, then we stopped at exactly the same time. We didn't know the rest of the words. We just looked at each other. I had never heard of the song 'Danny Boy' before I met AJ, and then he only sang a part of it, so I never really heard the full version until the marathon. I couldn't really get a handle on the words because it's written in such an old language and it's very Irish. It was a culture shock for Justin as well. He didn't know the song before either.

"For all the times I heard it, I guess my brain just caught the melody, not the words. I heard the music, but I didn't realize it was a funeral song, a sad song. I didn't grasp the words and the metaphors until Sunday.

"Then it clicked. It opened itself up to me. I could see it meant a lot to the people who were performing it. To see how people felt about that song was incredible. I didn't think it would garner as much attention as it did."

STEVE NEAVLING, AMBER HUNT AND GINA DAMRON filed more stories for the *Free Press* on March 15, 16, and 17. AJ recalls, "It was as if the media freight train had just turned the bend and was headed right for us. I was joking with Branden that I couldn't go anywhere without the paparazzi following me. I had done interviews with the press from Australia, Ireland, the United Kingdom, Canada, and the U.S."

DAN GREENE returned to the marathon Sunday and was again touched beyond words. "There were kids singing, and that let my emotions loose again. I just cried the whole time. I tried to hold it back, then I said, the hell with holding it back, go ahead and cry. When I saw AJ, I tried to tell him it was the best event I'd ever been to in my life, and I couldn't get it out because I was crying so hard."

Dan took the stage and managed to do his performance without tears. "There I was—number 620. When I was onstage, I was fine. The marathon was emotional, it was fun, it brought the community together, it was an accomplishment, and it was part of a dream."

AFTER SEEING THAT THE NOVI MAYOR could phone in a rendition of "Danny Boy," Stephanie Hall arranged a similar remote call-in from that evening's Novi Concert Band performance. She took the conductor's place at the podium, and told the audience about the world record. She put her cell phone on the conductor's stand, and the band played its booming brass arrangement. The audience cheered, and Stephanie says, "You could also hear the people at AJ's cheering through the phone. Even though we couldn't be in Ferndale, we were part of the Danny Boy Marathon."

GARY SENICK SAYS, "I walked in and I was blown away by how many people were there. No matter the level of musicianship, everybody was listened to, and appreciated for who they were and what they were doing.

"Just a wonderful event, just to be a part of it. The energy was so good, so high, and so positive, and it stayed that way all the way through. I talked to some friends about it—I think one of them played early in the morning and one of them played later in the evening—and they said it was always the same."

THE LANGSFORD MEN'S CHORUS was among the acts Gary remembers. Roger Smith, a member of the group, says that they used an arrangement by Al Youngton, one of its members, and they rehearsed it for the first time that evening. When they finished singing and the director brought his hands down, the crowd demanded an encore.

Roger says, "We sang the second verse again and this time it brought tears for many in attendance as well as in the group. Our chorus placed second in the International Musical Eisteddfod in northern Wales a few months later. Our Danny Boy Marathon experience helped us bond as a group and contributed to our success in the British Isles."

THERE WERE A FEW PEOPLE who stayed in the shadows but were part of the marathon, nonetheless. Joan, Kathy, and Courtney don't have addresses or phone numbers. They're not well dressed. Their social skills are lacking. They are homeless.

Joan waited outside, drifting in from time to time to ask AJ if he had any old bagels. "She's picky," says AJ. "She likes the salty ones." Joan was thin, and had been wearing the same dress for too many days.

When AJ first met her, she was filled with rage. He gave her a warm place and food when he could, and some of the other business owners did the same. "What she most appreciated," says AJ, "was when I gave her my ear. I listened to her rants, sometimes those of a woman gone mad. The school of hard knocks, harder than most of us will ever know, could make anyone insane."

Taking care not to loiter in any one spot too long, Kathy and Courtney spend some of their time at the park. If they have enough money, they ride the bus up and down Woodward Avenue.

Kathy wanted to sing, and so did Courtney. They meant to, and AJ told them they were welcome to, but they didn't. AJ says, "It's likely they were already embarrassed and didn't want to take a chance on being ridiculed or laughed at. No one would have done that, but their fear is easy to understand."

They mingled with the crowd, amazed at the attention their refuge was getting. They were as proud as anyone to be a part of AJ's Danny Boy Marathon.

TEN

SUNDAY NIGHT—A BOND OF LUNACY

"As it neared midnight," says Jim McLaughlin, "the number of people at the Café dwindled to 25 or 30, but I stayed to check people in anyway. Those dedicated folks took turns to ensure the marathon continued. Then it happened. The others needed a break, so with AJ's 'encouragement,' I got on stage with him— the first and only time I sat down during the marathon. Singing wasn't so bad after all."

Aoghain Lakes was there again that night. "These two young guys came in. They looked kind of like punk rockers, eyeliner on. Their style of music, it was just out of the... But they had a lot of energy."

It was Michael Langan's group, "Marco Polio and the Vaccines." They had a synthesizer and a drum machine and sang "Danny Boy" to their techno beat.

Mike Wilhelm remembers, "Around 3 in the morning, it started getting real, real wild. The techno guy did maybe five or six 'Danny Boys.' He had a sequencer and it was going, 'Dsh, dsh, da da, dsh dsh...' You could barely hear his voice. Then he'd get loud: 'DANNY BOOOOY, DANNY BOOOOY.' He didn't have a whole lot of melody, but it was interesting. The more I listened to it and tried to be open minded, the more it started getting through to me. That was what the 'Danny Boy' thing was all about, not being too worried about doing it in a traditional way. It was about doing it your own way—and he was doing it his own way."

"Other people started to get up and sing it the way these two guys were singing it," Aoghain continues. "Usually you associate stuff like that with heaps and heaps of alcohol. But everybody had just had a couple of cups of coffee and the caffeine was kicking in. It was just adults behaving like kids. Those two guys were up there and it was their music, their style, their way of life, and they shared it with us, they welcomed us to join in. It was just brilliant to be a part of it."

"After this went on for a while," says Mike, who was running the soundboard, "Keith Dalton told me it was time to get other people on. I didn't know how the performers were going to react, but I didn't even have to tell them. I just hinted that it was time to let some other people come up, and they packed up their stuff and were gone."

AJ WAS WONDERING if they would make it through Sunday night. He stayed awake as long as he could, ready to sing if he had to. When a group came in and said that they were prepared to take the stage for some time, Keith convinced him to go into the back room and take a nap.

"I had trusted him and the rest of my stalwart crew this long," AJ says, "I might as well take them up on it. If I could get a catnap in, I'd be sure to make it to the end. I went back to the office and turned on a TV to drown out the sound of the marathon and convince my brain to rest.

"I woke suddenly. I heard Edith Bunker singing 'Those

Were The Days' from *All In The Family*. I rushed out to the stage, only to find someone singing 'Danny Boy.' Later, Jim McLaughlin told me that someone had in fact sung like Edith Bunker while I slept."

IN THOSE EARLY MORNING HOURS, an elderly man with a walker came in with his harmonica. Mike says, "He couldn't manage getting onstage with the walker, so Keith turned the karaoke monitor around to face him. When the words came up, he kind of mumbled them. After he did that a couple of times, he started to feel empowered, and said he wanted to do a harmonica version. It was quickly clear that he knew very little about playing the harmonica, but it obviously came from his heart. You could tell he had to summon up the courage to do it."

MARY TERESA was there with her friends, Terry Bracken and Russ Smith, and recalls how singing the song affected Terry, "It was just such a good experience for him. He has such a nice voice, but not enough confidence. The first time he got up there alone, he was backing away from the microphone when it was time to belt."

As Terry grew more comfortable, he was part of one of the more inventive versions of "Danny Boy." As Mary describes it, "Terry went up with Russ and he felt more confident because he had somebody with him. He sounded marvelous, he didn't shake, and he didn't seem too nervous.

"In one version, he sang operatically, 'Oh Danny Boy...' and in Geico commercial style, Russ said, 'He's got a son named Dan.' And then Terry went, 'The pipes, the pipes are calling...' and Russ said, 'And he needs a plumber.' And for every single line of the song, Russ had some smart remark to go with it. Everybody was in stitches, everybody was absolutely hysterical."

"Then there was the sock puppet," says Mike. "We were definitely ripe for that kind of a presentation. Russ took off his boot, took off a sock, and formed it into a sock puppet. Then the sock puppet sang 'Danny Boy' in a creaky female voice. It was superb, just brilliant. Russ put a microphone in front of the sock puppet, and he sang into another one. I kept trying to turn the sock puppet's mic up instead of the puppeteer's."

A few months later, AJ ran into Russ. He told AJ that he had just returned from Ireland, and that he had sung "Danny Boy" in a pub there, bragging about being in the marathon. Russ chortled, "They had heard about it!"

MIKE AND OTHERS REMAINED vigilant, "There were times when there was nobody onstage, and one of us had to jump up there and do another version. It was a case of 'OK, let's see… what am I going to do this time? How am I going to change it up a little bit this time?'

"This led to things like an Elvis version—the Memphis Mafia Elvis, the later Elvis—and there was a Dracula version. 'Bruce Springsteen,' 'ABBA,' and 'Edith Bunker' were there too."

"You know, when you're up at 4 in the morning watching guys sing 'Danny Boy' like Count Dracula or Elvis, it creates a bond of lunacy," says Kevin Zanotti, defining the atmosphere perfectly.

TOM GAGNE LIVES a few blocks from the café. Knowing that Sunday night going into Monday morning was going to be a tough time, he told AJ on Sunday afternoon "Call me, no matter what time you need me. Let me know. I'll be ready."

He recalls, "I woke up around 4 in the morning and realized that the phone hadn't rung, so I threw on my clothes, put my hat on, picked up my guitar, and got over there.

"Later, I went over to AJ and said, 'I told you to call me.' He was kind of dazed. He said, 'I thought I did…I think I had a dream that I called you.' Well, I didn't answer the dream phone.

"We did 'Danny Boy' like Bob Dylan. We did a Bee Gees version, we all did it a capella. We started to do an Arlo Guthrie version that started out with the 'Alice's Restaurant' introduction. Mary was at the soundboard and she came running up, panicked because she thought we were actually going to sing 'Alice's Restaurant.' She was yelling, 'You can't sing that, you can't sing that!' As soon as we went, 'Oh Danny Boy…' you could see this huge sense of relief on her face. She thought we were going to screw up the entire thing."

Mike says, "I had worked out a kind of Appalachian banjo version. Tom liked it and he told me that when he went up, he wanted me to come and play the banjo part while he played guitar. We started out with the dueling banjos opening. Then we went into this hillbilly banjo/guitar 'Danny Boy.'

"Tom started calling other people to join us. First it was a trio and then it was a quartet. I think by the time we got finished, there were probably six people up there, doing it all sorts of different ways. Tom said, 'Hum it.' So we did a humming version. Then no guitars, just everybody's voices singing the lyrics. He was very inventive, he came up with a lot of different ways to do it."

"By the time I was playing for two or three hours," says Tom, "my fingers were so sore, it was so painful. Every time I'd play something, it just hurt, but because we were having such a ball, no one really cared that the guitar strings were buzzing or I missed a chord here or there. You just keep playing through it."

ELEVEN

SAINT PATRICK'S DAY

JUST BEFORE SHE TOOK HER CHILDREN to school, Tom Gagne's wife Tiffani called AJ and asked if there was anything she could do. There was. Dozens of green bagels were ready to be picked up at the New York Bagel Company.

"She arrived with the rising sun," says AJ, "with her child holding one hand and bags of green bagels in the other."

As Tiffani tells it, "Michael was in his jammies, boots, with his sippy cup, and people are yelling, 'Yaaay, new bodies! Come up!' And I'm like, I am not going up there, you've got to be kidding. But we did."

She says to Michael, "And you sang, didn't you? He didn't know all the words so he just kept going, 'Oh Danny Boy, oh Danny Boy...'"

Michael pipes up, "And I said 'Happy Saint Patrick's Day' real loud."

The Gagnes later found themselves being interviewed by CBC, Canadian public radio. Tiffani says, "Michael was very chatty. He's saying, 'He's having a marathon. We're trying to break a world record.' He knew exactly what to say. The interview was published online. Very exciting. Now he's been bugging us, 'Are we going to AJ's? Are we going to AJ's? Are we going to AJ's?'"

Tom and Michael Gagne.

THE BUS FROM THE SAINT PATRICK'S Senior Center arrived with eight elderly performers, men and women of every background and race. The agile mixed with the not-so-mobile.

AJ remembers one lady with special fondness, saying, "Mabel was old and without teeth. She was thin and almost surely living in a state of Alzheimer's. She didn't sing, but she did perform. She danced and grooved with the energy of the young Irish dancers who had opened the marathon. She was a girl again. The Irish hat she wore only added to her charm, throwing time and age out the window."

Scott Cleven, the center's director, says, "The seniors were so excited about performing, and it made it even more incredible when we arrived and there was a crew from Channel 7 waiting. Many of the seniors were interviewed. We performed a traditional version, and then a faster gospel version. Lou Finn, 83 years old, played his beautiful mandolin version."

No one would say that "Danny Boy" was somber if they had seen those seniors sing.

STEPHANIE LOVELESS, newspaper publisher and rock and roll performer was pulled in too. She says, "I stopped in to see how it was going. That's when Brian roped me into going on stage. He wouldn't take 'no' for an answer. I went up on stage with only the faintest grasp of the melody and words. I sang twice as fast as the karaoke. Finally, it was over, and the gracious and forgiving audience applauded.

"The funny thing was, although for the life of me I could not learn the melody in advance of the marathon, for the next three weeks I couldn't get it out of my head. I was humming it everywhere."

UP NEXT WAS ANOTHER in the long line of unfamiliar faces. She checked in with a weary AJ. Along with all the other volunteers, he was running on adrenaline now. Just get the performer up there, let them do their thing, then off the stage, and on to the next performance. Only two hours to go.

The marathon rules, which hadn't been mentioned all day, said that everyone had to preserve the integrity of the song. They could perform it any way they wanted, as long as they didn't change the words.

The woman rose to take her turn. She started to sing: "Oh George Bush, your days, your days, are numbered…"

Keith Dalton exploded, "Holy S*%&! She's f-ing up the song!" AJ, sitting next to Keith at the sound controls, thought at first it was just a different language. They'd been hearing Polish,

Yiddish, French, and other non-English versions throughout the last 48 hours. But at Keith's uproar, he realized what was happening. Keith muted the microphone. AJ rushed to remove her from the stage.

"I can't believe you did that," AJ was livid. "Can't you see the rules?" Some versions had varied from the standard, but the song had not been fundamentally changed—until now.

AJ told the woman that she might have ruined the whole thing. She'd have to live with screwing up the marathon.

"I was dismayed, upset, angry," he says. "I asked her to leave. Then I saw in her eyes that she was horrified. She was in tears. She simply didn't know the rule. She made a mistake, an innocent mistake. I felt awful. I hugged her."

Then AJ asked her, "Do you know what you can do for me? You can go right back up there and forget all about what just happened and sing your heart out. Sing the best 'Danny Boy' you can."

As she sang, Keith told AJ that her first performance had only lasted a few seconds. It wouldn't change the outcome of the marathon at all.

~⁊

SOMETHING BIG WAS ABOUT TO HAPPEN that afternoon. Andy Meisner was the first to hear about it. "Monday morning," he says, "I got a call on my cell phone from Governor Granholm. She said, 'Hey, Andy, What's going on with that "Danny Boy" thing?' I told her. And she's like, 'Is it still going on?' She was going to be in the area. I told her, 'Yeah, it's still going on, and we'd love to have you there.'"

Getting the Governor would make it more than a *Guinness*

Book of World Records attempt. "It's a little piece of Michigan history now," Andy says, "and it's clearly taken on a life of its own."

Men in dark suits came to the café around 1 pm and told AJ they wanted to look around. "I didn't know who these people were," AJ remembers, "but I knew they were official something. I thought it was the health department—that I was over capacity or something. I gave them a tour and they said, 'You're going to get a special visitor in 20 minutes. Don't tell anyone, but the Governor is on her way.'"

Although AJ had had no idea she was coming, about a month before the marathon, he had planted the idea. He had supplied coffee and Michigan cherry scones for a reception the governor attended. AJ had managed to talk to her for a moment and invited her to the marathon. Later, the governor's aide gave AJ her card, along with an empty plastic bag—would he please fill it up with scones? AJ had followed up with the aide, but never heard anything back. Then, the Friday before the marathon, he ran across the card and gave the aide a call.

Now that the mysterious men had visited, AJ heard rumblings from the press: "Is it true the governor is going to be here?"

"I didn't say that," he'd respond to each query. They wouldn't get the information from him.

Then Governor Jennifer Granholm appeared. AJ says, "It was such an honor. She was beautiful in her emerald green shawl. She's so vivacious and she has the best smile."

The governor told AJ, "I just want to say hi."

"You've got to sing now that you're here," he told her.

"I can't sing. I can't carry a note."

AJ reassured her, "Come on, I'll go with you."

She followed AJ to the stage as he took her by the hand. They started singing. AJ says, "I helped her—I made sure I was louder than she was, so if she needed to, she could follow my lead. She enjoyed it once she got going. You could see it on her face when the whole audience was singing with her."

When she signed the funeral book, she wrote, "Way to go!" She was given a T-shirt and a carnation. In answer to one reporter's question, she said, "I wasn't going to sing, but AJ is very persuasive."

Michigan Governor Jennifer Granholm and AJ O'Neil Governor Granholm told reporters, "AJ is very persuasive," after leading the crowd in a spirited rendition of "Danny Boy."

CHRIS KOLE WAS ONE OF THE WITNESSES. She says, "From my son's school, where I'm a lunch monitor, I went to AJ's, with mud still on my shoes from the playground. If it was possible, there was even more excitement in the room than there had been on Saturday.

"I sat in the on-deck circle and waited my turn. Then a slim, attractive blond woman was ushered past us to the stage. 'Who let her have cuts?' I whispered to the teacher sitting next to me, mimicking the kids in the lunchroom. Then we recognized her. It was our governor, Jennifer Granholm, with AJ. After a few words of congratulations and appreciation, she led us in singing 'Danny Boy.' Wow, Ferndale was the place to be.

"After my turn—in all, I sang a total of five times—I just sat and enjoyed. A father and son duo brought tears to our eyes, senior citizens dedicated the song to their parents from the 'auld sod,' people who physically couldn't get up the steps sat at the base of the stage, filling the room with the strength and depth of their voices.

"My favorite was the young African-American 'Saint Patrick,' complete with green bishop's hat, who blessed us before he began his quiet, classic instrumental version. Soon his solo turned jazzy and soul-filled, and he had us rocking and clapping. He blessed us again and exited the stage. He brought down the house."

Hour 50

BACK WHEN HE WAS FEVERISHLY compiling the master time slot sheet, putting in hundreds of names five minutes apart, AJ decided to reserve the last hour for close friends and people who had been instrumental in making the marathon happen.

Among the first people he called was Kyle Rasche, whose band, "A Stowaway," had played when NPR's Desiree Cooper recorded her feature. Kyle says, "The band—Dan Trevisan, Jonathon Ratliff, Chris Flynn, Andrew McLemore, and I—stopped to perform on our way to a gig. I had never seen the café that full, and everyone was in great spirits. AJ and the sound guys appeared to have been drinking coffee non-stop, and the line to the stage was buzzing with people ready to participate.

"It was one of the most fun musical performances of my life. We started mellow and traditional with two-part harmonies. The drum kicked in and we threw in a third vocal harmony for '... if you come when all the flowers are dying...' By the last chorus, the whole place was clapping and singing along with us. I looked at Jonathon halfway through the tune and we both had to keep from laughing because we were so surprised by the reaction. The audience was great. The atmosphere was electric. AJ was getting the attention he deserves. We walked away from the experience with 'From Glen to Glen' shirts, and great memories. Who knew that a little idea could blow up into such a production? AJ did."

"When I saw Butch Hollowell in line, it was a welcome sight," AJ remembers. "I felt good knowing he was there to help bring it all home, after he had pitched in to help us put the marathon together." In his gospel-inspired performance, what was most important to him, Butch says, was that his daughter was there to see him on stage.

AJ also wanted Tom Vesbit, current "Ferndale Idol" champ, to ask his Polish grandmother to sing in the final hour. Tom says, "I signed up on a whim when I met AJ, and signed my grandma up without her knowing. The energy was wonderful.

I loved it that such an event could bring out so many people.

"I was wearing my brightest, greenest shirt and tie. The real challenge was convincing my grandma to perform. She had translated the lyrics into Polish, and she had practiced, but once the time for the performance arrived, she was trying desperately to back out. I wouldn't let her. She sang and got a great response, especially from the Polish community. I loved watching her perform. She was nervous, but she got through it with flying—green—colors. I think it did wonders for her spirits. She still talks about it."

MARK KIRBY, A LONGTIME FRIEND from AJ's construction days, had called to get on board when that first *Free Press* article was published. AJ says, "The guy isn't the on-stage type and he can't sing at all, but he had asked me to put his name at the end to show he believed we'd reach our goal. My brother Bobby, my brother Dennis and his girlfriend, Melanie, and I got up there with Mark and helped him get the job done. Just another job for Mark, and he did it with stoicism and grit.

"Dennis is not the best singer either, and being on stage is not who Dennis is. But he did it. He practiced and practiced with Bobby, and he was determined to overcome stage fright and do his part."

Then, just as they had many times before, AJ and his three brothers stood together, this time to sing "Danny Boy." AJ says, "I helped Dennis, Dennis helped Bobby, Bobby helped Brian, and Brian helped me. You wouldn't see that—you would just see four brothers singing together. I thought of Pops as we sang, and imagined Heaven's keepers giving him a pat on the back. As he had on the last night of his life, he saw his four boys together in harmony."

Brian Londrow, Ted Berlinghof, AJ O'Neil, and Mike Wilhelm.
A triumphant AJ reached for a high note after fifty hours of
"Danny Boy."

ALMOST IN TEARS, Ted Berlinghof came to AJ in that final hour, saying, "AJ, I would be honored if I could go up there and do the last song with you."

"I was touched beyond anything," says AJ. "All we had been through and done together, and here was this lovable soul asking if he could sing with *me*. I was the one who was honored."

A few minutes later, an exhausted but victorious Brian Londrow asked AJ the same question, saying the same thing, "I would be honored."

"OK," AJ said, "You and me and Ted will do it together."

Then AJ saw Mike Wilhelm, who, along with Ted, had encouraged him to go on stage and sing "Danny Boy" that first time. Mike not only believed in AJ and his "Danny Boy" dream, he worked tirelessly to help accomplish it. AJ says, "I asked him to join Brian and Ted in helping me sing the very last 'Danny Boy.'"

Finale

BRANDEN WAS WORKING THE COFFEE counter then and recalls, "I wasn't paying attention to what was happening on the other side of the house, because we were so busy. All of a sudden, it just stopped. What was going on? I looked around the corner and saw everyone watching the stage."

"Now we were bringing the song home," remembers AJ. "I had sung the first 'Danny Boy' 50 hours earlier, and now it was time to do the last. So it was Ted Berlinghof, Brian Londrow, Mike Wilhelm, and me who had the enviable honor. Two fine guitarists and a piano virtuoso, playing as I sang. I motioned to the crowd and everyone erupted, '...Oh Danny Boy, oh Danny Boy, I love you so...'"

Branden was touched and remembers vividly, "When they started singing, you really felt the passion. It was a collective passion. It was so beautiful. It was the last hurrah."

"By God, we did it!" AJ said to himself. "We made it non-stop for the whole time, and achieved our goal and a world record."

In the crowd, people felt exuberance, relief, victory, accomplishment, and joy. The final signature was logged into the sympathy registry and it was brought up to the stage.

AJ asked for the Irish flag. To the crowd, he said, "I'm sure my dad is getting a kick out of this. And God bless you all for these memories."

From the crowd came, "God bless you, AJ!" and applause.

As he waited for the flag to be brought, AJ said, "The world watched us and the world was overcome with joy. I don't think this will ever be called a depressing song again."

Brian Londrow handed him the toy-sized flag. AJ was given the book and he placed the flag on top of it, saying, "And now Reverend Deb Dysert…"

Reverend Dysert began, "My grandparents were both born in Ireland…"

When she ended her short "service," AJ led the audience in singing "Danny Boy" one last time.

It was over.

The crowd began to drift away. Some people didn't seem to be able to leave, staying behind in groups, chatting and reliving the high points. "Danny Boy" had lived in that café for so many hours, people felt the loss. A few more interviews were recorded for TV and the newspapers.

AJ and Branden went home and had pizza—not corned beef—with Annie, Dennis and Bobby. "I was the first one to hit the sack," AJ says. And just as he crawled into bed, AJ remembered he had to be up early for a Chamber of Commerce meeting at 7 am.

KEITH DALTON, one of the many workers who made the marathon possible, said, "No matter what you hear now, at the start no one had a clue that we would go worldwide. We knew we would get good press and radio around town and regionally, but then CNN picked up the video from our local station. When that happened, instantly we were worldwide. And I mean the world—Peking, Sidney, New York, Boston, Moscow, Capetown, Dublin, London, LA, Miami, Mexico City, Rio."

Scott Cleven, who'd never written a press release before, sent one out letting people know that the marathon had hit the 50-hour mark. The AP picked it up, and like the story of the banning of "Danny Boy," it appeared all over the world.

News of the marathon had reached China, India, South Africa, Russia, Thailand, Austria, Australia, the UK, and beyond. Video news stories had appeared all over the United States, Canada, India, and Europe on nightly news, Web news, CNN, MSNBC, Fox, and others. The marathon was included as "Weird news happenings" in the *Washington Post*. Bloggers worldwide weighed in.

The *Detroit News*, *Detroit Free Press*, *Royal Oak Daily Tribune*, *Between the Lines*, *Woodward Talk*, and *Ferndale Friends* sent reporters. Fox News, WJBK, WXYZ, and WDIV TV, and WWJ, WOMC, and WJR radio did updates and live interviews with guests and performers. The Saint Patrick's Senior Center performers had the thrill of seeing themselves on the 6 pm news on Channel 7. AJ says, "It seemed like everyone got on TV or in someone's newscast. We loved the attention. The lucky reporters who were there when Governor Jennifer Granholm showed up got a real scoop."

By Monday, March 17, London's *Sun* and *Metro* had brought word to the British that the Irish in Michigan were celebrating at AJ's Café. The *Metro* explained that, in America, on Saint Patrick's Day, "...it is traditional for anybody who's ever been to Ireland, enjoyed a U2 song, or owned a dog called Seamus to proudly proclaim their Irishness." It seems like they missed the point.

And, believe it or not, *Ripley's Believe it or Not* called the day after the marathon requesting information and pictures.

Twelve

Say an "Ave" there for me

Perhaps it was because AJ talked of singing "Danny Boy" at his dad's funeral. Maybe it was memories of it being sung at countless others. It could have been the mournful words and haunting melody. Whatever it was, there were many people experiencing grief as the marathon unfolded. It was as though AJ had given them permission to remember and talk about those they missed so much. For many, tears were mixed with elation during hours of hearing the sentimental Irish song.

Dorothy Crawford's husband Robert loved "Danny Boy." She knew he would have loved every minute of the marathon. But in 2002, they learned that Robert was developing a malignant brain tumor. "We had no idea that he had any problems at all," Dorothy says. "We were at a dinner dance two nights before I called 911. He lived barely two months longer."

Robert had been a teacher and a high school principal. "When they heard of his illness, we had students coming in and out of the house, day and night. Many knew how much Robert loved 'Danny Boy.' One man played it on the horn for him.

"Hospice said he would not make it through Christmas, but he had great determination. He passed away December 28. We had Robert's memorial service a couple of weeks later. One of the ministers has a magnificent tenor voice and he sang 'Danny Boy.' We also had a piper and, after a piper plays, he walks away and the sound gradually dissipates.

"After that day, every time I heard 'Danny Boy,' I had to leave the room. If it was playing on the radio, I would turn it off. As much as loved it, I could not listen to it. I would break into tears, and remove myself from the room the minute I heard the first chord.

"I told my grief group, which has supported me through the years since Robert's death, that I had heard that AJ was doing a marathon at his coffee house. 'I want to be there for it,' I said, 'but I don't want to go alone.' My friends told me, 'You don't have to, because we're going to go with you.' So we went."

AJ remembers meeting Dorothy, a petite lady who reminded him of his grandmother, saying, "Her red hair and sweet smile were those of a real Irish lass."

A few days before the marathon, she had come into the café and told AJ her story about what "Danny Boy" meant to her. AJ says, "She told me that she would never be able to hear the song again, or at least that's what she felt at the time, but she thought the marathon idea was great. She wanted to help.

"Every day after that, she came to the café, going back and forth in her mind about coming to the marathon. Every chance I got, I encouraged her to do it. I think I nearly had her persuaded to sing. A couple of days before the marathon, she said that she was going to do it with her support group. I hugged her and we went to the master time slot sheet to sign her up."

On the day before the marathon, however, she called AJ and said she would not be able to go through with it. AJ told her he understood, and hoped that she could at least come as a spectator. She did.

Dorothy says, "When the first chords of 'Danny Boy' were about to come, I took a newspaper and put it up in front of my face. By the time we got to the end, I was handling it."

Dorothy and her friends didn't expect to stay late but they did. They also didn't plan to go back there on Sunday, but found themselves there anyway.

AJ says, "Dorothy is one of hundreds of new friends in my life, and that has been the biggest blessing, by far, to come from the marathon. I was so warmed to see her there, sometimes attentive to the performance, sometimes in a world only she and her husband would know. This was one of the countless heartwarming stories to come from the Danny Boy Marathon."

"I wasn't going to go over on Monday," Dorothy continues, "but as I was debating about it, the phone rang. My friend Jean was there and she said, 'Dorothy, get yourself down here. This is the day they're having the funeral, and the governor is coming.' I missed the governor by about 10 minutes.

"I called another friend, and said, 'Linda, you have got to get yourself down here.' She said, 'I'm at work and I can't leave.' I said, 'Well, tell your boss what's happening and see what you can work out.' She didn't think he'd agree, but I said, 'Try it.' She did, and all of a sudden she appeared.

"We stayed on through all of the music again. We were there for the funeral when it ended. As we were walking back to our cars, we said we would never, ever want to hear 'Danny Boy' again.

"Well, I sang 'Danny Boy' all the way home, and I sang it

in the evening. When I saw the girls at our meeting the next night, I said, 'I have been singing "Danny Boy" ever since I left. I thought I would never sing it again.' It was strange how it had this power over us."

WHEN TEY MEYER FIRST HEARD about the Danny Boy Marathon, he was skeptical. "I'm not Irish," he says. "I'm Romanian and German. But I did all this research about the song, about the author, and where it came from, and that brought meaning to the song for me. Then I was more than willing to perform it.

"After the passing last year of the person I was dating, I was able to understand the lyrics. This concept of loss, and dealing with loss, and managing loss is what brought meaning for me, because I've been going through that myself."

Tey first performed "Danny Boy" as a weepy Edith Piaf, and then gave it the full Wagnerian operatic treatment. Knowing that other people had their losses and that the song is about facing death, Tey says, brought healing, "A lot of people that I spoke to during the event would tell me how much this song meant to them, because they heard it at their uncle's or grandparent's or a spouse's funeral. We were able to bond because we've all lost loved ones, and this song relates to that feeling. It helps you to get through the loss."

KEVIN CALLAGHAN GREW UP in a family surrounded by music. His parents had met at a musical, fallen in love, married, and had 18 children. Kevin says he was lucky number 13. He says, "Every year for several years my family has had an Irish party that raises money for vocal scholarships. It was there that my niece Maura told me about the attempt at the record for 'Danny Boy.' I got thinking about my dad's recent passing at age 91.

"I was in his choir for 30-plus years. Singing was like breathing—it was just there. It didn't matter the situation or the song. I just did it—no fear. But somehow over the years I got stage fright.

"My dad fell on January 17, 2008. I went to the hospital and several of my siblings were there. His final words were, 'I love you guys.' At the cemetery, next to my mom and my sister Ann, my dad was laid to rest. My niece sang 'Danny Boy,' but it wasn't going so well. So in support, folks started humming and then we broke into song. I let it rip, just like AJ did for his dad, and the send-off was beautiful.

"When I went to AJ's Café on Saint Patrick's Day, I was nervous, I walked through the place and heard some, well, hard-on-the-ears stuff. For me, that was encouraging. I was sixth in line, shaking in fear, but I heard even worse singing. I said to a lady watching, 'I just lost my stage fright.'"

Kevin took the stage, number 967 on the master time slot sheet, and it was clear to him what he needed to say, "I dedicate this to my father, who art in heaven—two months and two hours ago."

HUSBAND AND WIFE Jeff Jahr and Judy Moon have performed on-stage for years, including appearances at open mics at AJ's. They hadn't been out much lately, however. Jeff came to the open mic alone a few times. He never said why Judy wasn't with him or why he sat in the back writing in his notebook.

He and Judy had suffered the loss of their child, and their grief was still raw. Judy says, "Our little five-year-old, Grahm, passed away Christmas Eve."

Jeff had learned about the marathon at one of the open mics and he signed up to help. He says, "We had weeks in advance to get ready, but it was only a couple of days before the marathon that we bought the CD and listened to it. We were almost to the point of saying, 'Let's not do this,' but we spent the whole day rehearsing it."

"It was a tough day," Judy says. "I was in a very tough grief day, but we both had signed up. It was a commitment and so we'd follow through with it. When it was our turn to sing and we came to the part, 'Come ye back...' I got hit with the emotion of it. I didn't expect it. I almost started crying right there, but I somehow got through it."

Jeff didn't. He says, "By the time the song was done, I had already lost it."

"While we were rehearsing, I was just rehearsing it mechanically," Judy recalls, "but here I got into the emotions of it, and then it really touched me. I heard that one woman playing had had a child that passed away, and the couple next to us talked about someone else who had passed away and how 'Danny Boy' had meant something to him. I think what hit me was the combination of my feelings for my son and emotions ricocheting back from other people.

"I felt like Grahm's spirit was with us. Sharing with others—everybody has a story—when I listened to a few of those stories, it brought more sincerity to it. When we got off the stage, a friend I hadn't seen in years grabbed us and said, 'Oh my gosh. I can't believe that you guys sang the song so close to your son's...' Just the connection of her knowing, and just the respect that she had that we sang the song—"

Jeff says he was covered in tears as he signed the book. He says, "When we came in here, when we walked into the energy—"

Judy interrupts, "It was a wonderful thing. It was amazing, and to be there and to feel that energy, with our grief for our son, and to be able to share that—"

"That was much more than I expected," continues Jeff. "It was a great experience. I'm still trying to figure out what the tears were about. It unlocked something. We were in a different place after we left."

"A very powerful, very moving thing," says Judy. "AJ told us about his father, that he sang 'Danny Boy' at the funeral, so just the idea of him singing at his dad's funeral and putting this marathon together was touching. Being there for the marathon helped us. We were so glad we did it.

"It's a song that touches so many people, and when you have your own personal feeling, it makes it...we were really happy to do it. I know Grahm would have been happy—he *was* happy."

AJ REMEMBERS THAT HIS FRIEND Robert Johnson had seemed to be in a fog in the months before the marathon. Robert says, "We had lost our Sarah—only 15—in January. AJ invited me, along with Big Ed Berger, and John Salizs, the Robert Johnson Blues Band, to compose and perform a blues version of 'Danny Boy' for the event. For me, it was just what the doctor ordered. We dedicated our performance to Sarah's memory. Thank you, AJ, for touching so many lives in such a thoughtful, thoughtful way."

THIRTEEN

OUT OF MANY, ONE

"IT'S THE HUMAN ELEMENT, it's dedication, it's belief in miracles." That's what Kris McLonis says of the marathon's success.

AJ HADN'T SET OUT to create something spiritual. At the beginning, he was reaching out to the community to get enough singers to perform and to promote his business. If he could get people into his café once, some of them would become regular customers.

As the momentum grew, however, he began to understand the spirit that surrounded the café. The community had a center, and it happened to be AJ's Café. The marathon reaffirmed that, and built upon it. This wasn't an official community center like city hall or the town's recreation building. It was like the counter at the diner in one town or another town's donut shop, where you went to learn the important things, like how Frank's garden was doing, or whether kids' Little League baseball should be competitive or just for fun. Maybe learn who was moving back home from San Francisco. Or tell everyone that you now had a new grandchild.

ANDY MEISNER FEELS the Danny Boy Marathon was a blessing for the community. He says, "Anything that can bring people together, and get people from different backgrounds together, with a common purpose, a shared mission, is really special."

Poet Sparrow Karas says the marathon reflected what is really ordinary in human beings, but seems extraordinary because we don't experience it often. She believes that every moment in our lives can be like that.

"There was an earnestness and a heartfelt level of engagement that can be very rare on planet Earth," she says. "The half-dozen or so people who preceded my dog Sonny and me on stage were of varying ages and so-called singing abilities, and everyone approached it with a similar respect. No one was flippant or joking or just doing it for the heck of it. Their investment was obvious and very touching. It was like a crystallized dose of for-real humanity. People just did their best. It was wonderful what it brought out in everybody. It was a sacred happening."

For Tey Meyer, "It was exhilarating to have this crowd of people getting together as a community, no matter what their differences were. We all shared in this moment and became one. And that is because of AJ and Branden and their vision for the café. They want it to bring people together, so we become a community, learning from each other. That's what the experience became for me. It was, wow, all these people that I never met before and they're here for the same thing I am. It was very uplifting."

THINKING OF ALL THE DIFFERENT PEOPLE she saw, Dorothy Crawford says, "You could have had a basketball game, you could have had a bridge game, you could have had euchre and cribbage. You had teenyboppers, preschoolers, and people who were up in years, every age group that you could possibly think of. You had people from just about every walk of life. You had people of every race.

"You had people of every nationality. As we say, you do not

have to be Irish to celebrate Saint Patrick's day. Everybody is Irish on Saint Patrick's Day. And that day at AJ's, everybody was Irish."

Dorothy saw a community of people engaged in one thing. "You could see tears once in a while. It probably reminded people of what it reminded me of," she says, thinking of the loss of her husband, Robert, who loved the song so much. "And then you saw laughter and fun."

"WHAT'S SO UNIQUE about AJ's is how positive it is there," says Josh Richart, a customer and open-mic player. "No matter who you are, you always feel welcomed and accepted. You feel it when you walk in. Those 50 hours were that day-to-day philosophy on a much larger scale. People who would probably never meet, would never cross paths—this brought them together for one really crazy thing. Just seeing the power of people—I think AJ is very influential at making you care about something."

MIKE WILHELM REFLECTS, "One thing that struck me was how different all the versions were. You don't really think about how different people are, how they all see things from a different perspective, but when we were doing 'Danny Boy,' it came out. Everybody brought something out of themselves and put it up on stage. It was a wonderful thing to see, everybody bringing their own slant to it. We had people come up who were not really great musicians and didn't have great voices but they always brought something really special."

BRIAN LONDROW HAS VIVID MEMORIES of seeing the event come together. "What an event and what a way to draw together the community–not only in Ferndale, but across the globe. My first thought was 'This is going to be an organizational mess' but as it developed, I leaned toward thinking, 'We really need this.' This was a great way for people to come together and focus on the power of unity.

"It was exciting as the event drew near to see the multitude of people signing up and the diversity which each person was going to bring to the song. This was the social impact of the event. It didn't matter who each person was, what the journey was, socio-economic status, religion, sexuality, or political stance.

"There were those who could have peeled paint off a building with their singing. It didn't matter. It still added color to the whole picture. There were those with polished talents, and their performances were equally important. It was not a competition. Everyone received the same enthusiastic response. People would stay for hours listening. Collectively, the event showed how we can be if we only set our sights on what is truly important."

～

AJ HAD WANTED TO SHOWCASE his neighbors and what their businesses had to offer visitors. A large out-of town contingent would be in Ferndale, and it would be an opportunity for them to discover the other great shops, restaurants, and entertainment spots there.

Some businesses signed on as sponsors. Others couldn't spare the $200 for it. AJ got together with the city's Downtown Development Authority (DDA) and came up with a way for all of them to get involved. The DDA made up postcards with the names of dozens of neighborhood businesses surrounding a big green shamrock. If a shamrock appeared in their storefront window, they were offering Danny Boy Marathon specials and discounts.

Cristina Sheppard-Decius, Ferndale DDA executive director, says, "What started as a quirky idea to drum up business during a very cold, hard winter exploded into an amazing community-spirited event that drew attention from across the world. Metro Detroit could not wait to sing its heart out, and the excitement mounted with each passing day. People came from far and wide.

"AJ worked night and day to make this event a success, and he succeeded. He was able to not only make a mark for his business, but also help others in the community with charitable giving. It is part of AJ's heart to give back, which is why everyone can't help but like him. He is the type of person that makes everyone feel welcome, no matter who you are, where you've come from, or where you're going.

"AJ's was the place to be on Saint Patrick's Day, and it became a true draw for Downtown Ferndale. Ferndale is honored to have AJ's Café as one of its businesses, and we expect many more innovative ideas from him. Creativity is the backbone of Ferndale, and AJ's Café exemplifies that."

ONLY FOUR SQUARE MILES IN SIZE, tiny Ferndale is separated from Detroit by Eight Mile Road. One side of the road doesn't look much different from the other. Ferndale shares the gritty realism of Detroit, and its ability to endure adversity.

The next city north of Ferndale is Royal Oak, an artsy home to hipsters and singles. Shopping and dining are becoming more and more upscale in Royal Oak. Ferndale has its share of artists and writers, and remains more down to earth, less spoiled by commercialism. Families find Ferndale neighborly.

Ferndale's position between the two larger cities attracts an unusually diverse population and AJ's Café has become a microcosm of the region. It is a place where well-dressed suburban ladies chat easily with gay couples, where white, black, and Asian people blend together, and the very old mingle with the very young.

AJ HAS STRONG FEELINGS about Ferndale's potential. He's an idealist, but also a business owner and is well aware of the need to continue improving the city's appeal. He says, "I think the Danny Boy Marathon showed Ferndale that it *can* be a universally welcoming town. Just like AJ's 'reserves the right to serve everyone,' so can Ferndale. Our edginess, combined with our suburban neighborhood feel and our creativity and diversity, makes things like our marathon work.

"People flocked to Ferndale for our marathon and many shopkeepers told me they did well. My neighbor, Jim Monahan from the Twisted Shamrock, said that it was his best weekend ever.

"With the city and the residents continuing to work together, people will come into town, not just for a Danny Boy Marathon, a pub crawl, or a festival, and then leave. They will return often. They will want to be a part of a town that is a model of diversity, and where we respect every person's right to their own journey. Ferndale has its challenges. We have tough economic conditions right now. We have some boarded-up storefronts. Anchor stores like Old Navy have left.

"Even so, the *Metro Times*, Detroit's top alternative newspaper, ranked Ferndale #1 in all of Metro Detroit as the place to dine for 2008, ahead of Royal Oak and other popular areas like Greektown, Mexicantown, and Birmingham.

"Ferndale is alive and ready to go. Heart, wit, grit, love, laughter and a little madness—that might describe Ferndale and everyone who lives, visits, and finds their voice here. And that may be why the Danny Boy Marathon could take off in Ferndale and not anywhere else."

DAN GREENE SEES A LITTLE BIT of New Orleans in Ferndale, saying, "In fact, it *is* New Orleans without the drinking. When I lived there as a young man, I didn't really appreciate the culture, the architecture, the beauty. Now AJ's represents creativity to me, with all the artwork on the walls, the huge variety of music. The musicians who come in there. And the poets. AJ is open to that kind of stuff and he encourages it. We need more people like him. AJ's may be the epicenter—maybe ten years from now this will be what Ferndale is known for, all of this creativity."

WHEN MIKO STEINBERG WAS ON STAGE, he told the crowd about the drum circle that convenes there every Sunday evening, and invited everyone to come back in a week and join the circle. The drum circle now has several new drummers.

Miko says, "The Danny Boy Marathon, because of the people behind it and the energy it grabbed, it's the reason I live here. It was the community at its best. Neighbors seeing neighbors. There was no division, it was complete diversity. We had the men's choir coming here, we had a couple singing in drag, we had transgender people here, we had people from different nations singing. The event was a serious culmination of everything that this community stands for."

ALAN STURT BELIEVES that some people have the enthusiasm that makes impossible things happen. "AJ is one of those people," he says. "When he first told me of his Danny Boy Marathon plan and asked me to sign up I thought he was nuts—it will take so much organization—you'll need so many people. But AJ pulled it all together, making it a real community effort. So my hat's off to him. It leaves me wondering—what's next? What other world records will be set here—in Ferndale—right in our own community?"

Behind these doors, crowds received performance after performance of "Danny Boy" with appreciation and warm applause.

Fourteen

Breath of the Soul

In AJ's life, there has always been song. Annie O'Neil, says, "I sang all the time at home. I used to throw the kids in the tub every night at 7:30. I would sing at the top of my lungs. I didn't know it, but the woman next door—she was close to 90— would come up on the porch every night to hear me sing.

"I sang, 'Three little men in a tub, scrub-a-dub-dub,' and then I just started singing any old song. My husband and I liked the song, 'Oh, how we danced on the night we were wed.' I'd sing them songs like that." Raising four boys is a challenge. When times are tough for parents, Annie has this advice: "You have to sing."

Ted Berlinghof has a philosophy about singing and a grudge against canned music. He concedes that, because some of the greatest performers of the past have recorded, we can hear them, but he thinks modern performers do a lot of the same thing, crank it out and sell it. "For millions of years, human beings have made their own music," he says, "but now we're told to go out to the CD store and buy this latest CD by so-and-so, or download it on your iPod, and go around and listen to it, and that's how to enjoy music. People get the message that they can't sing, they should never perform, and they should listen to the music that is being sold to them."

As an open mic host, Ted encourages people to make music themselves, and he says it's a revelation. They say they can't do it, but if he can get someone to get up on the stage, and give them a little encouragement, they find they can do it. They can sing.

"THERE WERE PEOPLE WHO HAD terrible voices who had the courage to get up and sing," says Dorothy Crawford. "We all applauded and applauded for them. It's something that they probably wanted to do all their life, to be on stage and perform, and they never had the opportunity. And then they heard all these people clapping for them."

Song has always been an important part of Dorothy Crawford's life. Her beloved Robert, however, never felt he could join in. "In my family, we love to sing," she says, "but when Robert was in first grade, his teacher told him not to sing because he was throwing the rest of the children off. And it crushed him. He would never sing, and yet he loved music. He just relished it when our daughter Pam and I would sing while she played the guitar. I don't know if we were that good, but he loved it.

"Maybe we could have gotten Robert to sing 'Danny Boy.' We'll never know that, will we? But maybe he *was* singing it. How do we know?"

HEARING "DANNY BOY" the way AJ sings it touched Dan Greene. "About a year before the marathon," he says, "I went over to the café to catch the Wednesday open mic, and got there just in time for AJ to sing 'Danny Boy' for the first time at his place. As soon as I heard that song, the tears started."

It was the singing more than the song itself that got Dan. He says, "I think it was my inner child responding to those few times when my childhood was good. My dad was a very stern man, he was not very loving or nurturing. But he did sing 'Danny Boy' to me when I was very young. And AJ brought it back. Singing at the open mics—that was me asking my inner child what he enjoyed. It's music. Making people happy."

"THERE IS SOMETHING BEAUTIFUL about amateurs performing sincerely," says Greg Sumner. "As people perform, we all expose something. There was something tender in the performances at the Danny Boy Marathon, maybe because of the song. People showed a kind of vulnerability. In this day and age when amateur singing tends to be like 'American Idol,' you have to be really, really good to feel like you can even open your mouth.

"The marathon was a very democratic experience in that you didn't have to be technically skilled. You just had to bring a sort of spirit. And everybody I saw brought that spirit. In some ways, the more shy, rough around the edges, or amateur-ish people appeared, I liked it all the better."

From Bangladesh to Ferndale, a breath of soul

BRIAN O'NEIL REFLECTS, "The spirit of any song lives on through its singing, generation after generation. Just think of all the people the marathon touched who were inspired to keep singing 'Danny Boy,' and how many people will now pass it on through future generations, and even to other cultures."

ABUL HASSAIN WRITES AND PERFORMS poetry and song, accompanying himself on the ektara he made. It's a timeless instrument—just a gourd, some bamboo, and a string—though friends have added a pickup and electrified it. Abul has one foot in antiquity and one foot in the now. He writes poems about our loss of humanity and the need for love and peace, and blends them into traditional songs from Bangladesh. "I write poetry in English. I do song in my language, Bengali," he says.

"When I came to open mic, AJ told me, we do 'Danny Boy' for Saint Patrick's Day. He told me this is a celebration of Irish; it is an Irish song. He give me the tune. Ancient, ancient song. Very old song. This ancient tune was a real singing tune, the singer does from the heart. From heart, so it is a natural thing. I heard it, I like it. I am excited, that's why I do song.

"I do not understand the words of song. But the voice of song, tune of song, is a wonderful song. There is some very deep thought inside the 'Danny Boy' song. Song is very deep song.

"Song is a breath of soul. Not an exhausted breath, or tragic breath, or a joyful breath, it is a breath of soul. Whether sorrow or joy. Sorrow, we have to think about. Joy, we do. We ask, 'Why he cry?' And joy—no matter what, we can do joy.

"And really, it is a tragic song, but I like this song, because this song keeps going on. Myself and so many people not know about this song, many American people. But this year, this year, 'Danny Boy' is at AJ's. I think, maybe thousand people learning this song. All day long it was. People sit down and they listen. Only one song, they listen all the time. And it is very beautiful thing for everybody. They do not feel any bad, they do not feel any exhaustion. I saw a lot of people again and again singing. Same thing. But nobody exhausted or nobody feel bad. That means people want this thing.

"So our song, 'Danny Boy,' keep going on, three days, and everybody realize what is this song, and we enjoy, we enjoy. We do joy, and sorrow. And keep our humanity."

FIFTEEN

THE SPIRIT OF "DANNY BOY" LIVES

I need a Guinness—not!

AFTER THE MARATHON, AJ went on to re-register the feat with Guinness. He had no doubt that the world record for the longest continuous singing marathon was now held by AJ's Café, although he saw on the Guinness web site that a singing marathon of 40 consecutive hours in India had been recognized. AJ says, "We had whupped them by ten hours."

He breezed through the application and paid $600 to have it fast-tracked and $57 more to fax it. A reply came within two days. AJ is still flabbergasted, "They said they didn't have a category for the marathon, and they had no interest in creating a new one."

The rules used in the Indian marathon were so different that it was impossible fit the Danny Boy Marathon into the same category. Some of the requirements were:

- Songs could not be repeated
- No one could perform more than once
- A doctor had to be on hand for the entire event

Now when people ask, AJ tells them that Guinness doesn't want to have anything to do with the marathon at AJ's Café. "But no one can take our record away," he says. "They can't take away what mattered most, coming together as one huge family to put something magical together. We had the entire world rooting for us and it felt great. We don't need Guinness to validate that. We are the world record holder for the longest Danny Boy Marathon, Guinness or not."

THE PEOPLE WHO WERE PART of the marathon haven't seemed to care about the *Guinness Book of World Records* either. AJ's Café is an emotional landmark for them now, where they can expect to find welcome and friendship.

For Mary Teresa, "AJ's is like a community place now. It's a great place to meet. It's a great place to hang out. The marathon was my immersion in Ferndale. I've been back for open mics several times."

It is part of Dan Greene's life. "I live 25 miles away, but since the marathon, I've been at AJ's at least once a week, sometimes two or three times," he says. "It's my favorite place. It's my hangout. I love it. I like the people there. On Wednesday nights, I take my guitar and perform at the open mics, along with Ted and Mike and Greg, our poet Sparrow, and Alison with her cello."

When he talks about the future of AJ's Café, Miko Steinberg sees great potential. "The more publicity there is," he says, "the more people will come to Ferndale, and when it comes to publicity, AJ's not afraid to just go out and grab it. Who else would have gotten the governor to come here? Do I want to see this place always be the hub that it is? Sure. Do I want to see AJ prosper and not compromise his serenity? Absolutely. Do I want the people who come here to be touched by the magic that we're touched by every day? Without a doubt. I want this place to always be a beacon. If people know that a place like AJ's is here, and if 'Danny Boy' brings some recognition, draws a light to this place, then people are going to want to come live here. And I want that."

KRIS McLONIS LOOKS to the future, saying, "A lot of people are wondering what AJ has up his sleeve for Saint Patrick's Day next year. Are we going to try breaking our own record? Or perhaps do another Irish song? Are we going to have a dance marathon with Michael Flatley, or Riverdance?

Ted Berlinghof says that after the marathon ended, "AJ came up to me—he was totally stoked—and said, 'We gotta do this again next year.' My reaction was, 'Oh God, no, please...' But he was ready."

Greg Sumner thinks there might just be a return of the Danny Boy Marathon. "We're ready to follow the pied piper again," he says. "I don't think I could stand another 50 hours of 'Danny Boy' right now, but maybe by next March I'll be ready for it. The networks that have been built up—let's keep building on them. The hardest work was building the network in the first place. Now it's in place."

Fame

A FEW DAYS AFTER THE MARATHON, AJ headed for Key West to get away from "Danny Boy" and the lingering Michigan winter. "But 'Danny Boy' popped in where I least expected him," says AJ. "I was talking with a couple from Chicago. 'I'm here to get a break after our Danny Boy Marathon,' I told them. 'Oh, you're the guy from Detroit,' they said. 'We saw you on

TV in Chicago.' Pretty neat."

On his way home, AJ was in the Tampa airport. Among the people waiting to board the plane were some girls from Michigan. "You're the 'Danny Boy' guy, aren't you?" one of them asked. AJ answered, "Why yes, yes I am."

Branden says that people have been coming in, saying, "Oh, you guys did the 'Danny Boy' thing." People have read about it and want to see the café that held the Danny Boy Marathon. The café has become a tourist spot.

A couple came in one day, and AJ introduced himself, as he always does when he sees newcomers. They were from Manhattan. AJ says, "When I told them they were in the place that had the Danny Boy Marathon, their eyes lit up."

"OH MY GOD! I CAN'T BELIEVE IT!" the woman had exclaimed. Foley's Pub was in their neighborhood in New York and they knew about the marathon. They told AJ they couldn't wait to tell their friends that they had been to AJ's Café.

AJ's BRAINSTORMS DIDN'T STOP with "Danny Boy." The Michigan Primary for the Presidential election went awry for the Democrats. It was not sanctioned, but Hillary Clinton campaigned, put her name on the ballot, and won unopposed. Her team said that gave her Michigan's delegates. Others disagreed. The Democratic Party was divided.

AJ decided he would hold a mock primary. He emphasized that it was an unscientific, unofficial election that would have no ramifications for the nomination process. When the ballots were counted, Barack Obama had won. AJ's Café endorsed him.

A few days later, AJ and Branden went to one of Barack Obama's invitation-only town hall meetings—without an invitation. AJ took along Senator Obama's "prize" for winning—Harry Truman's book, *Plain Speaking*. He says, "It was my own copy. I had written all sorts of notes in the margins when I read it. I figured it might be a way to get my opinions to Senator Obama."

Dressed in an old T-shirt and work pants that had seen better days, AJ approached a campaign worker. He told him about the "primary" and gave him the book for later metal-detecting and dog-sniffing.

AJ and Branden were ushered to a place in the front row. Senator Obama then selected him to ask the first question. AJ says, "I plugged the café and our primary before I asked him, 'How do you think you'll do in Michigan?' After the meeting Senator Obama shook my hand and said he would like to get to AJ's Café to 'check it out some time.'"

From the mayor of Ferndale, to the governor of Michigan, to a presidential candidate, AJ seems to have free access to people in politics.

AJ's Café held more special events, some of them pretty goofy. There was a "Singing in the Shower" one Saturday. People who claim that the shower is the only place they sing had that excuse taken away. AJ built a working shower on the stage and dozens took their turns—in bathing suits—singing as they were soaked. Hundreds were there to witness it and so were the TV cameras and newspaper reporters.

Some events were initiated by veterans of the marathon. Dan Greene organized an open mic night where only Bob Dylan songs could be played. It filled the café. Mike Wilhelm and Greg Sumner instigated a Beatles open mic that brought an even bigger crowd.

MICHIGAN IS WOOING HOLLYWOOD, offering hefty incentives for shooting movies in the state. Pacing outside AJ's one day was Drew Barrymore. She was directing scenes being shot two doors away from the café for her movie about roller derby girls. Ellen Page and extras on roller skates came in for coffee. A couple of the crew members came to an open mic one night to treat Ferndale to some LA rock.

AJ has been worming his way into movies as an extra since he struck up a conversation with a woman who turned out to be a location scout. Cuba Gooding, Jr. was in Detroit to shoot scenes for his film about the pediatric neurosurgeon, Ben Carson, who worked his way from ghetto to operating room. AJ spent a day on set with Gooding, impersonating a German doctor.

AJ pitches the café to every Hollywood denizen he meets.

FOR THE HOLIDAYS, AJ WROTE "The Birth of Baby Jesus in Ferndale," a musical comedy with a message. It portrayed Mary and Joseph as a homeless couple dealing with an unexpected pregnancy—the birth taking place at AJ's Café—and shared its earnings with the Gleaners Community Food Bank. Some of the same people who helped propel the Danny Boy Marathon to its finish—Butch Hollowell, Mary Teresa, Russ Smith, Dan Greene, Mike Wilhelm, Brian Londrow, and Keith Dalton—once again organized themselves into a production team. Butch's daughter, Desiree Hollowell, joined the cast and a few new friends were drawn into AJ's web. The audience for the sold-out premiere included Governor Jennifer Granholm and her family. Once again, the press picked up on the event.

~~~

THERE SEEMS TO BE NO END to AJ's imagination when it comes to making the café a place that brings people together and supports the community. But, most of all, it's a place where you can count on getting a warm welcome along with your hot coffee.

INSPIRATION

Sparrow's poem

*the
centrifugal
force of
AJ's
enthusiasm
compelled the
likes of
shy-me to
dang well get
up on that
stage and
follow the
bouncing ball on the
karaoke machine (heck
I didn't know those O-
Danny-Boy
lyrics.) twas a*

*truly sweet
event with
each person's
rendition so
skillful so
sincere so
heartwarmingly
precious yes twas
Sunday
mornin' when
me'n my dog
Sonny we
got up on
stage together for
our turn
(AJ chiming
in to give me courage)
YIPPEE!*

—SPARROW KARAS

Tales of "Danny Boy"

While traveling in Ireland
in two-thousand-one,
we went pub crawling,
for porter, music, and fun.

At a pub in Blarney, some
musicians dropped in.
The sound of their music
quieted the din.

They played of the troubles,
they played of old loves.
We sat and enjoyed it.
We were quiet as doves.

The guitarist next to me
was as big as a giant.
He put down his guitar
and picked up his pint.

So I asked why, after all the
songs we had heard
We did not hear "Danny Boy"
We heard not a word.

He looked at me, a giant with
a tear in his eye.
He said, the boys feel they
Can't do it justice,
and neither can I.

—JACK GUIREY

The pipes, the pipes are calling

On a clear day...or not so clear, on a blustery day even,
on any day that yields no rain,

I can hear from my window the pipes,

The pipes, they call me from down the road,
a block and a house away from mine own,
the unmistakable sweet pipes of Arthur,
who won't give in to a Michigan chill
or a curmudgeonly neighbor and he plays.

With a sip of his Scotch and his kilt proper, he plays.

Oh, he blows and wails, and fine tunes will come
from his ancient, tentacled bag.

And for me, for me, and me alone, I like to think,
he will play "Danny Boy."

He is a trucker in the night who did not know me from Adam
Until his Storm and I met one day through the fences,
gathering our curious and and wandering dogs.

Is that your mutt? Storm says. Why yes it is, I say,
and Buddy, he be yours? Aye, she says,
And that is my man who blows the pipes
when he returns to me from the journey, from the road.

It is sweet to my ears, I tell her, very sweet indeed.
Stop by the Café and grace us with your pipes,
won't you pass that on to your mate? I ask her.
And she does.

One day, out of the blue he does, he does blow up
to the great Danny Boy Marathon and he blows those pipes.
He and many more pipes they blow.
The pipers, they know "Danny Boy."

For them, "Danny Boy" is the tying-your-shoe of songs.
You learn it and when you do, you never forget it
and can bring it back again, anytime again like a
breath of fresh Celtic air.

Ask a piper and he'll tell you

He and his breath and "Danny Boy" are one.

—AJ O'NEIL

NOTES

Luck of the Irish

THE IRISH SAY THAT SAINT PATRICK is a source of luck. According legend, he was kidnapped in Britain and enslaved by Niall of the Nine Hostages. The Irish conqueror and warrior was the forbear of the O'Neils, O'Neals, O'Neills, and all those with other spellings of AJ O'Neil's name. How lucky is that? It may be a long thread, but Saint Patrick and AJ O'Neil are connected.

AJ also has a historical connection to "Danny Boy." A song associated with the old tune was "O'Cahan's Lament." The O'Neills and O'Cahans have a long history of both conflict and connection with each other. For a time, the O'Cahans were part of the O'Neill clan. In what is now Northern Ireland, they were allied in fierce resistance to English domination. See Bardon, J. (1992). *A History of Ulster.* Belfast, Ireland, The Blackstaff Press.

~~⌒

Origins of "Danny Boy"

THE ANCIENT TUNE FIRST PLAYED for Rory Dall O'Cahan by the fairies was passed from harper to harper, and was eventually played by the fiddlers of the Roe Valley. In 1851, among many of those preserving the ancient airs of Ireland, Jane Ross took down the tune as it was played by Jimmy McCurry in the town of Limavady in the County of Londonderry (now Derry).

Some dispute the accuracy of her transcription. Whether it was McCurry who played it in 4/4 time or Miss Ross's mistake, when the song is played in 3/4 time, it is "Aislean an Oigfear" or "Young Man's Dream," collected by Edward Bunting in the 1790s.

The words sung to the original tune were variations on a fantasy of a young man about his vision of a maiden. One version of "A Young Man's Dream" goes:

> *One night I dreamed I lay most easy*
> *down by a murmuring riverside*
> *whose lovely banks were clad with daisies*
> *and the streams did gently glide.*
>
> *These sudden raptures of delusion*
> *lulled with slumber sweet ease*
> *I thought I saw my lovely Susan*
> *through the green and the blooming shades.*
>
> *O then I fancied she drew near me*
> *With a melting and blushing air*
> *And by her countenance seemed to fear me*
> *And soon repented that she came there.*
>
> *Then I arose and gently eased her*
> *Whilst my charmer swooned away*
> *And in my arms I straight conveyed her*
> *To the arbor where I lay.*
>
> *She soon recovered her sense and said, "Sir,*
> *Why will you kill me? I am undone.*
> *Why will you smother a harmless maid?*
> *Pray let me go for I must be gone."*

Then in my arms with amorous kisses
I caressed the sobbing dame
And in the midst of all these blisses
I woke and found it to be a dream.

"Danny Boy" lovers interested in the history of the song owe a debt of gratitude to Jim Hunter, in Limavady, in Northern Ireland, for his research, publications, and his website, "The Origin of Danny Boy." See: http://www.theoriginofdannyboy.com.

Michael Robinson, musician, and author of the Standing Stones website, tells some stories about Danny Boy's origins and includes a midi sound file of the original tune. See: http://www.standingstones.com/dannyboy.html

Another source of information about the origins of the Londonderry Air and Danny Boy can be found on Nationmaster.com, at

http://www.nationmaster.com/encyclopedia/Londonderry-Air

A WORD FROM THE AUTHOR

AJ LIKES TO SAY that life comes to you if you let it, and that is exactly what led to the writing of this book. My husband Mike began playing the guitar at the age of 14, but never in public, only for family or friends. It was his friend Marilyn Schmidt who pushed Mike into going to a meeting of the Detroit Folklore Society.

Ted Berlinghof, leader of the group, then lured Mike to an open mic at AJ's. I went along with Mike, giving him wifely support as he braved the new world of performing on stage. I don't play an instrument or sing, but performers need an audience. Some nights I was an audience of one.

As AJ and I got to know each other, I learned that he had once written a yet-unpublished novel and he learned that I had had a career in publishing. That's why, after the marathon, he asked me for help with the book he thought should be written. Drawn into AJ's way of making unlikely things happen, I agreed.

I could tell that the story of the marathon was much more than an account of an event. The first glimmer of the significance of the marathon came to me when my son, Chris Samp, alerted me from Hong Kong that the story about Shaun Clancy's ban on "Danny Boy" and AJ's Danny Boy Marathon had hit the media worldwide. Then immediately after the event, I began to hear people talk over and over again about the feelings of connection and community it had awakened.

It's hard to think of myself as the author of *In Sunlight or in Shadow,* because all I did was listen to the stories of the real authors and retell them. Dozens of people who were part of the marathon sent written accounts of their experiences, and I recorded interviews with more than 30 others, including Dennis,

Bob, and Annie O'Neil. Just as all these people made the Danny Boy Marathon a success, their stories put flesh on the bones of this book. It owes much of its heart to them.

AJ O'Neil spent countless hours telling me of his life, his family, his beliefs, and his café. Much of his story fell outside the scope of this book, but it should be said that he has experienced adversity that is hard to imagine, and he has always been sustained by his optimism and faith.

As we worked together on this book, I learned how much AJ credits his parents and brothers Brian, Dennis, and Bobby for their support during his trials and his achievements. I join him in thanking all his friends at the open mics, his regular customers, and everyone who performed in or made up the audience at AJ's Danny Boy Marathon, who thereby made priceless contributions to this book.

Several people reviewed early drafts of portions of the book and provided counsel. They included Phyllis Barrett, English and writing teacher and a friend since junior high school, my brother John McWhorter, who advised me to "murder my lovelies," and my sister Diane McWhorter, who sent detailed notes from a reader's perspective. Gary Senick, an experienced editor of first-time authors' work, came through with his guidance.

The Wednesday and Thursday open mic crews listened to readings of a few passages, responding with encouragement about completing the book.

Michael Illitch read the first chapter and sent AJ a letter saying he had enjoyed the tender story. Baseball Hall of Famer, Ernie Harwell was exceedingly kind in connecting AJ with Bill Haney. Bill has been a true mentor, with his frequent reminders to do what's best for the book. He recommended that we change the focus of the book, and that required rewriting the whole thing.

He was right. It told the compelling story much more clearly. We knew we were getting somewhere when Marcy Haney read a draft she was able to call "a real grabber."

Saving *In Sunlight or in Shadow* from being merely a "book-like thing," Bill assembled a collegial publishing team of experienced professionals willing to meet the tight deadlines required to get the book out before Saint Patrick's Day, 2009.

Joe Simko enlivened the book with his illustrations, many based on pictures contributed by Bernie LaFramboise and Keith Dalton.

Good book design is rarely noticed. It never calls attention to itself; it just reveals the story. Jacinta Calcut gave us a number of font and layout styles until we found what we believed would best do that.

William Boardman combed the final draft, saving us from making many mistakes and providing some finishing touches.

Finally, the Thomson-Shore team showed what their continuous improvement and lean manufacturing practices can do to compress the time it typically takes to transform digital files into printed books.

Most of all, this book owes its existence to my husband, Mike, whose music has always opened doors.

Karen Wilhelm
February 2009

ABOUT THE AUTHOR

Karen Wilhelm is a freelance writer and blogger. *In Sunlight or in Shadow* is her first book. Karen lives outside Detroit with her husband, Mike.